Falling Forward

A Novel

A Novel

RJ Stastny

iUniverse, Inc.
Bloomington

Falling Forward
A Novel

iUniverse books may be ordered through booksellers or by contacting:

iUniverse
1663 Liberty Drive
Bloomington, IN 47403
www.iuniverse.com
1-800-Authors (1-800-288-4677)

ISBN: 978-1-4697-8325-3 (sc)
ISBN: 978-1-4697-8327-7 (hc)
ISBN: 978-1-4697-8326-0 (e)

Library of Congress Control Number: 2012903385

Printed in the United States of America

iUniverse rev. date: 03/01/2012

For Danny

Contents

֍ ֍ ֍

Prologue

⩊ ⩊ ⩊

L eaping like a jackrabbit, the topless jeep sped along a remote dirt road, and somewhere in the dark and musty Colombian jungle, it carried us against our will to a destination that we had no time to contemplate. The ropes around our waists that bound us to the seats kept us from escaping as well as from being ejected while we bounced through the darkness. The straps that bound my hands to the back of the front seat cut into my wrists as the jeep hurled from side to side. Tree branches, wet from jungle showers, raked over us, forcing us to keep our heads down. We traveled so fast that my blindfold began to slide up my forehead so that I could open my eyes, but the empty darkness brought me no further clues as to where I was or why I was there. I could only see the backs of the two men in the front, who I assumed were the men who abducted us.

"Let us go, please. Don't hurt us. Please don't hurt us! We haven't done anything!" cried the other captive, whose identity I didn't know. Overcome with fear, he was in a panic, sobbing and yelling. I was frightened as well, but when I tried to call out, I had no voice. Minutes earlier, I had been having a drink after work at a local tavern. Now we were captives on a hellish ride. I didn't know why they kidnapped either one of us or what fate we were to suffer.

During the quick moments of our abduction, before we were blindfolded, I noticed the two captors were wearing muddy boots and fatigue-like pants. One wore a military-looking shirt, the other a white tank top. They said little to us. There were only a few other patrons in the bar. Perhaps accustomed to this sort violence, they offered no assistance to us. It happened so quickly we didn't have time to resist.

Suddenly, the jeep slowed down enough that the wind no longer limited my vision or my hearing. There were moments when the bright moonlight pierced through the rainclouds that intermittently poured down on us. The guy next to me still had his blindfold on. He had stopped screaming, his head bent over as if he was passed out or frozen in fear.

I didn't know whether the musty smell came from the jungle or from our unshaven and sweaty abductors. Sitting in front with their backs to me, I could see that both had tattoos on their necks. It looked like two letters, a "D" and "C." I tried to listen to what they were saying. It seemed like they were arguing, but I couldn't make out but a few words. Unfortunately, those I understood didn't bode well for our futures: "echamos de esta basura"—"let's get rid of this garbage"—referring to us. Suddenly, the jeep came to a complete stop. Like at the end of a wild roller coaster ride, I was glad it had ended so I could catch my breath. But I was uncertain what would happen next. My eyes were burning and my vision was blurred. They came around the back, untied my captive companion, and took him away. I sat there, still bound, listening to the jungle get oddly quiet. *Boom! Boom! Boom!* Three rapid shots of gunfire broke the silence, startling me so much that I pulled against the restraints so suddenly that they cut into both my wrists.

Within minutes, the two men got back in the jeep. I could only imagine the fate of my seatmate. The wild ride continued with me alone in the back seat. We traveled what seemed like a half hour, my capturers not saying a word, at least any that I could hear during that noisy race through the jungle. What struck me in what should have been a moment of terror was that I didn't do a fast rewind of my life like many claim they have done during life-threatening experiences. Instead, I was paralyzed by curiosity. Why was this happening? There must've been some logical reason for me being here. Suddenly, the jeep stopped. The silence of the jungle once again dominated my senses. My kidnappers jumped out of the jeep and opened the door on my side. One of them untied my restraints and motioned for me to get out. The moonlight cast broad shadows beneath the jungle canopy. All of a sudden, one of them pointed to a path heading into the jungle and yelled, "Corre! Corre, mierda ... Run! Run, you piece of crap." I started to run. I moved like I was waist-deep in pudding. I didn't look back. Shots were fired. I felt them whiz by me and heard the *ping! ping!* of bullets ricocheting off the trees. I wondered if the next round would find me. I ran and ran.

PART I:
FALLING

One:

⑅ ⑅ ⑅

Las Vegas, Nevada—Present Day

The clock by the bed silently flashes 7:30 a.m. The early morning light pierces the sheer curtains, and a slight desert breeze makes them gently billow like a ship's sails. The dry air and morning quiet reminds me again that I am in the desert. Having moved from LA nearly twelve months ago, I'm no longer in the clutches of urban sprawl, odd-smelling air, and a constant hum of humanity doing whatever humanity does.

For a long while, I would wake up from that nightmare sweating and breathing hard, but it's been many months since its last visit. Now, if I'm to wake up out of breath, it will be due to the man lying next to me.

There's a familiar sense of warmth, and a musty yet sweet smell makes me feel secure under the sheets. A year ago, the man cuddled up next to me would have been an unlikely candidate for a permanent bedmate. This handsome, strong, and passionate lover is still sound asleep, his back and firm, round butt pressing against me as if searching out warmth and protection from the unfriendly world outside. My arm is wrapped around him with my hand resting near his muscular chest. With my head cradled on the back of his neck, the smell of his moist body keeps me aroused, but I just remain still and savor the moment.

Life is good. I'm not analyzing why things happen; instead, I just want to experience and enjoy again what I have gone without for so long. I've always embraced change, but it was usually initiated by me. Now, my life can best be described as a blend of certainty and chance, the planned and the unpredictable. A recent series of unanticipated challenges over which I had little if any control has dramatically changed my course. My life was turned upside down. I struggled to get back up, and when I returned to vertical, the horizon was unfamiliar.

There is a tattoo on my left forearm. It contains the image of a compass with the latitude and longitude of my hometown, Chicago, in the middle. On the edge are inscribed the words "Fall forward." In the past when I've fallen down, I've tried to face toward the future rather than backward into the past. While not always successful, it's what drives me now to build something new while still preserving some of the precious things left from the past.

Above me on the bedpost hangs a gold chain with a small, round locket the size of a nickel. I reach up and grab it, trying not to wake up the sweet and gentle man lying beside me. I open it, revealing a small compass inside. It was a gift from someone who was once a stranger, intending to remind me of where I had been and, hopefully, the new direction toward which I was heading.

This story is about the people and events that carried me through a journey of loss, discovery, redemption, and love. I wasn't looking to change myself. Rather, I was seeking an alternative view of the world, through a different lens. In this way, I hoped to redefine myself. How did I get to this place in my life—a new job, a new city, thrown back into the unfamiliar world of dating, and in bed with a man who helped me rediscover feelings I thought had been buried for good?

Here my story begins, twelve months ago.

Two:

⁌ ⁌ ⁌

Los Angeles—Twelve Months Earlier

I had been in Los Angeles for almost twenty years. The city had been good to me, providing exciting career opportunities, many good friends, and several boyfriends. Of course, many of my friends were lost to AIDS during that time, leaving a void that would probably never be completely filled.

I was told I looked younger than my forty-two years despite a light field of gray that invaded my short dark brown hair and trimmed goatee. As a former college swimmer, my six-foot frame was still trim and toned. I was proud of the state record I held in the one-hundred-meter butterfly, if only for that one year. I remember that even back then my chest and legs had more hair than the other guys. The coach asked one of them to help me shave once before a meet. It may have been the first time another guy shaved me, but it wouldn't be the last. Since college I had become a gym rat, bulking up a bit and getting more definition in the places the seemed to matter to a young gay man looking for love. As a child, I always had a baby face, something I deplored but others found cute. I envied the other guys who were beginning to look like men. I secretly wished I had a scar on my face to make me look more masculine or menacing. I guess the baby face paid dividends, as getting older left me with a youthful but more masculine appearance. I still appeared more innocent than I actually was and kept my bad boy behavior—along with a few tats—under wraps. In private I could reveal a wild side that often came as a surprise to unsuspecting dates.

Born Wesley Robert Svoboda of parents with Czech ancestry, I grew up in a Czech neighborhood in Chicago's Berwyn area. My father was a construction contractor, my mother a teacher. My father didn't learn English until he was in elementary school. He spoke Czech only occasionally at home but would often speak it with older friends—and especially with waitresses at his favorite Czech restaurant. Both were hardworking individuals. Having struggled in the Depression years, like many parents of that generation, they worked hard to provide those things for my sister and I that weren't available to them. I wouldn't say we were spoiled, but we certainly didn't want for anything. While the ethnic neighborhoods in Chicago had gone through much transformation in recent years, I treasured the fond memories of the Czech businesses that dominated the main thoroughfares of the neighborhood.

After growing up in a relatively insulated ethnic neighborhood, I was motivated to explore the world apart from the Bohemian bakeries, restaurants, and tightknit family gatherings. I was proud of my heritage but longed to get a good education and to experience the adventures that up through middle school I had only read about. I was grateful to my parents for supporting whatever path I chose. After graduating from the University of Wisconsin with the odd combination of a BA in botany and an MBA, I returned to Chicago. I took a job in a bank until I could find something related to my field of study. A year later, I accepted a full-time position with the California Department of Natural Resources working with ecologists and eco-scientists to help manage the business of preserving native plant species in the face of rapid commercial development. It was a rare opportunity to combine my love of botany with business. I had interned one summer at the Desert Studies Center in the Mojave Desert while in school. As the idea of creating state and national preserves in desert, coastal, and mountain regions was gaining both public and political support, job opportunities became more numerous, and I gladly accepted the chance to combine my interests in native plant life and business planning.

After seven years working for the state, I found opportunities to do independent consulting with firms and municipal and state agencies who wanted to do development near ecologically challenged or endangered areas. One opportunity led me to accept a "mission" with the United Nations in Ecuador for a year. I worked with the government in strategizing and implementing plans to minimize the impact of tourism on the environment and on native plant life, specifically. While I was only one of dozens of consultants on that project, it was rewarding to be part of such a large effort, and it afforded me the chance to live and work abroad. What resulted in being one of the great adventures in my life also proved to be an experience that would have an unexpected impact on me long after moving back to the United States.

❖   ❖   ❖

While in Los Angeles, I had several boyfriends. Only two developed into serious, long-term relationships. The first one lasted five years. He was an outgoing Cuban who introduced me to Caribbean culture, as well as to the sexual freedoms that were emerging within the gay scene. Though we were very much in love, it was an "open" relationship that included three-ways and bathhouses. That such a relationship would eventually fade was almost predetermined. He later moved back to Miami to help resettle family. We remained friends, but our lives grew in different directions. I was grateful for his encouragement to realize my dream to live and work abroad. A few years later, I accepted the mission with the United Nations in Ecuador.

I was with my second partner, Kevin, for nearly ten years. Shortly after returning from Ecuador, we met at the gym, a gym that he would end up managing and owning years later. He was a short, rugged, very proud African American man a few years my junior. He was generous beyond his means and wasn't shy about showing his intolerance for disrespectful and ignorant people. Through his eyes, I saw subtle manifestations of discrimination first hand. When we would eat out, the server would often bring the check directly to me. When making a large purchase together like a car or appliance, many salespeople would make eye contact only with me. From him I learned not to tolerate intolerance and not always to turn the other cheek.

We completed one another's sentences and enjoyed long road trips where we could talk about anything, and anybody. We gave one another a light kiss before leaving for work and another before going to sleep. While life, at times, became routine, we never took one another for granted. We never stopped loving one another, and we fully expected to live the remainder of our lives together. How wrong we were to assume we were really in control of our destiny.

During a weekend trip to Palm Springs, where we often went to escape crowds of LA, I noticed he lacked energy and complained of aches in his legs. It was very unlike him to have aches and pains, let alone complain about them. After several weeks, he went to the doctor, assuming it was some form of arthritis. After that doctor's visit, our lives would never be the same. X-rays revealed something suspicious in the lungs. After an unsuccessful surgery, chemo started. Nine months later, I was planning his funeral.

After Kevin's death, I felt as though my life had been turned upside down. We had been like two trees growing together—when one was cut down, the other was bare on one side. I felt exposed, half of what I used to be. Over the years, I also had lost a number of close friends to AIDS. I felt claustrophobic from the loss and absence of too many people. I knew that I needed a change. Even though LA had been a fertile place for me professionally and socially and I was left with a small core of generous and loving friends, I felt that my life's direction had been permanently altered. I was fortunate that by this time my consulting work and UN experience in South America had left me with some good business contacts. One of these contacts was the US Bureau of Land Management. I was offered a contract in Nevada to work with BLM to educate and help managers and staffers structure their efforts more strategically. Though it was only a one-year contract, I felt it was the open door I needed to make a dramatic change in my life. The BLM was no stranger to controversy, whether it was sale of pristine land to developers or the controversial reduction in the wild horse population in the western United States. But BLM land surrounded the Las Vegas valley and most of the Mojave Desert, offering what I presumed could be almost unlimited work opportunities. Besides, the prospect of spending more time working in the desert was appealing. After all, it's where I got my first internship after college, and it was like a second home to me. Anticipating my move, I quickly completed two small consulting contracts I had in LA. I was hopeful that the BLM contract would provide me some foundation for security in a move where everything else would be uncertain.

The house in Los Angeles sold quickly, and I bought a run-down ranch home on an acre of barren land on the outskirts of Las Vegas. It was open and airy, and the location was quiet, with 360-degree views of the mountains. It was going to be my dream house landscaped with a variety of native desert trees, bushes, and cacti. I rented a small bungalow in LA for three months while the house in Las Vegas was renovated. While I wasn't enamored with the casino strip area of Sin City, the raw beauty of the surrounding landscape could be quite remarkable. The ready access to wilderness areas of the desert, mountains, and Colorado River was unmatched. Las Vegas was close to LA but far enough to make me feel I had made a major change. Some friends tried to talk me into moving to Palm Springs. Yes, PS was beautiful and had an organized gay community, but I wasn't eager to move to a desert extension of LA. I wanted some solitude, and more importantly, the feeling that I had separated myself emotionally and physically from the past. My friends would tease me that the move to my "retirement" house was going to happen much sooner than I had ever expected.

❖   ❖   ❖

At Kevin's funeral, I wasn't surprised by the large number of people who came to pay their respects. There were at least two hundred friends and relatives. Kevin had impacted a lot of people. I was deeply touched. Among those many well-wishers were several dear friends: Angelo, my best friend and confidant who I had known since high school in Chicago; Daphne, a friend I met through Angelo; the unlikely duo of Clay, a black man who has spent his adult life advocating for LGBT issues, and his partner, Matthew, a white conservative from upstate New York; Emil, the youngest and most flamboyant member of our "family"; and Jesse, a former coworker and straight friend of Kevin, who had befriended me shortly after Kevin became ill. Familiar with my propensity to make big changes, my friends were cautiously supportive of plans to move to Las Vegas.

Several days after the funeral, Angelo, a well-known bass guitar player and leader of his own band, took me out to dinner at a Thai restaurant in Studio City. Having spent most days as caregiver, I hadn't been in a restaurant in nearly a year. I felt like I had been released from prison. It was a sad and happy occasion—sad about the absence of my partner, and happy to have the social interaction I so desperately needed. Angelo always seemed to know what I needed and when. I had never felt more grateful for a friend like him than during that time.

My friends all agreed to maintain our "family" dinner that we had shared each year for the past ten years. The dinner was a way to keep us all connected at a time when we were all following different paths in our careers and relationships. We cancelled the past year's dinner to due Kevin's illness. I volunteered to host the next one. It would continue to be a small group of five or six: me, Angelo, his date if he was so inclined, Clay, Matthew, Daphne, and Emil.

The experience of losing a long-term partner in such a tragic way changed my perspective on life. I was no stranger to loss, but this was more significant. It came at a time when I naively thought I knew what I'd be doing for the rest of my life. The universe suddenly changed the balance of things. It put me in a suspended state, feeling lost and living without a visible horizon. I wanted to renew my enthusiasm for adventure and the future and avoid becoming a spectator. It was important to remain an active player in the game, but the rules of the game had changed. I was anxious, but I wanted to play again.

Three:

♪♪ ♪♪ ♪♪

Departure/Arrival

I was caught off guard when Jesse insisted that he wanted to help me move. He was straight, after all, and up to then had been only a work friend of Kevin's. I didn't really get to know him until Kevin became ill. I thought I was just a collateral friendship. He continued to surprise me after Kevin's passing when he wanted to stay connected. I knew he was deeply hurt by the loss of his good friend, one of the few people he would say showed him respect. Angelo, who originally had planned to help me move, was on a tour date with his band in Europe. I told him I'd probably need his support more once I was in Las Vegas.

Jesse had a challenging and troubled life. He never finished high school, was a teenage father out of wedlock, had been a dancer at a strip club and an escort for female clients, and was briefly incarcerated for auto theft. Despite what would have been a downward spiral for many young men with that kind of baggage, Jesse found redemption in his short stay in prison and earned his GED, and the warm, generous, and loyal qualities that were always part of him surfaced and flourished. He worked hard, reconciled with his children, and even got married to a nice young professional woman. He appeared to be making a good life for himself as an airport shuttle driver.

Although he liked to display his street savvy and ladies' man persona, he was bright, creative, and extremely sensitive. He was about ten years younger than I was, but had an uncanny sense of pride and common sense and a deep respect for and loyalty to those who treated him as an equal. I think he took a liking to me because, as a well-educated man who had all the advantages that he didn't have, I never looked down on him and always showed him that same respect and loyalty.

I remember when Jesse came to the funeral home the evening before the services. I was alone in the funeral parlor. He went off by himself and wept. I was deeply moved. We didn't talk much but he kept me company the rest of the evening.

I enjoyed the fact that Angelo, a career musician, and Jesse, a former male escort and stripper, had unconventional careers and backgrounds. Both were men of integrity, intelligence, and honesty, but they complemented my more conservative background. While they let me live vicariously through their very different lives, they in turn appreciated my more traditional and secure lifestyle. We were loyal friends and the universe had done me a great favor in making them part of my life.

Jesse came the day before the move and helped to load the truck with the remaining furniture and items that had not already been driven out during my many weekend trips. He arrived that morning bristling with energy. He clearly appeared to be on a mission. Exhausted from packing and the gauntlet of good-byes that I had to endure, I felt like he was heaven-sent.

When I opened the front door, Jesse had his signature grin on his face. "Hey, DB. Ya ready to get this sucker loaded up?"

Jesse had started to call me DB. I asked him "What's the significance of DB, Jessie?"

He responded with a smile, "Da Boy!"

It would have sounded odd from anyone else, but the way he said it was sexy and endearing.

We started to take everything out of the house and stack it up in the driveway, but when it came to loading the truck, he immediately took control of the situation. He took his role seriously and with such pride. He packed the truck so tightly that there wasn't even room for a throw pillow. I felt a strange comfort in relinquishing control to him, perhaps fantasizing that the control was over more than just loading the truck.

Watching the sweat roll down his face, I said, "Jesse, I feel guilty with you doing all the work. Why don't you let—"

He cut me off. "Ya don't understand, DB. I want to do this. Trust me. This is the way it should be." He stood up straight with his chest puffed out.

When we finished, we shared a couple of beers. He quickly devoured the pizza I had ordered.

Before leaving, he hugged me, and his eyes were filled with compassion from what he must have imagined I was feeling. "DB, we'll get ya where ya need to be. I'll be right there with ya, ok?"

He had crossed the line from being just a friend of Kevin's to being my close friend. I felt a warm rush inside. He headed back home. He did have a wife and young son, after all, and agreed to come back early the next morning to drive with me to Las Vegas.

❖　❖　❖

Even though I was an early riser, Jesse showed up earlier than I had expected. I thought I'd have some time to sit in the back yard and digest the big change I was about to make. But I was happy to see him.

"Mornin', DB. Ya ready to haul out? I already had breakfast, so whenever ya ready, I'm good to go."

Jesse took off his work shirt, his white tank top clinging to his muscular torso.

Seeing how eager he was to get going, I responded, "Sure, I'll be ready in a few minutes. I can't thank you enough, Jesse, for helping me out. It means a lot, and of course, Kevin would have appreciated it too."

"It's a'ight, man. We doing it for him too." There was a clear sense of pride in his voice.

I'll never forget the ride out of LA that morning. Jesse drove the moving truck with the car towed behind. I felt numb, having just said my good-byes to friends and work associates, many of whom, despite mutual promises to stay in touch, I knew I would not see again. I felt sad but not sorry about leaving LA. After all, the city had been good to me and supported several good careers. It was there I was fortunate to have experienced a loving partnership and to have made lifelong bonds with intelligent and inspiring friends. My heart pounded softly as we got further and further away from the LA basin. As we approached the Cajón Pass, the final ascent over the San Bernardino mountains into the Mojave Desert, my breathing grew more rapid and a light sweat broke out on my neck and forehead. *Cajón* in Spanish translates to "box", the shape of the steep and winding pass surrounded on all sides by tall mountains. How ironic that during that last year in LA I had felt boxed in, trapped by loss, and smothered by routine and familiarity that at one time had been comforting. Passage through the "box" canyon that morning was a profound symbol of escape and a new beginning. But I was scared.

As we climbed up the pass to the four-thousand-foot summit, I promised myself I wouldn't look back. But I did. Through the truck's large side mirror, I could see the beautifully sculpted canyons and snow-capped mountain peaks with the hazy topped LA basin below. I had made that trip dozens of times before, but this time I knew I was leaving behind a large piece of my past. As we reached the summit and the car leveled off, a vast horizon appeared, surrounding us on all sides. Joshua trees lined the highway like sentinels guarding the entrance to a different world. Directly ahead, the orange-pink sunrise cast a glow over the sandy and rocky landscape, the air fresh and the sky unblemished by clouds.

I watched as the horizon reappeared over each mountain range, but it was what I couldn't see that scared me: my future.

I exhaled. I wept. I smiled. I could feel Kevin's presence. I think he was telling me it was okay.

Jesse, aware that I had been quietly crying, inquired in a soft tone, "Hey, ya okay, man?"

"Yeah, I'm good. I knew this part of the trip would be tough. It's a fire I need to pass through." I was trying to be stoic, yet my voice crackled as I spoke.

"Ya gonna be fine, my brother." He gave me a quick squeeze on the leg with his strong, thick hand.

Unusual for a straight man, he felt no awkwardness in touching or hugging. I often wondered if he was bi or just one of those rare men who felt secure and comfortable in his own skin. I always assumed the latter but secretly fantasized about the former.

Even though Jesse loved to talk, he sensed I needed some space to absorb what was happening. We didn't say much through the four-and-a-half-hour trip. I never grew tired of the desert scenery and the unblemished landscape. Few people realized what diversity and surprises were contained in what to most looked like empty sand and rock piles. I looked at the desert landscape, the bajadas and playas, through a different lens this time. The so-called falling sand dunes, so named because they were created from sand blowing up, over and down the mountain sides as opposed to a more typical dune created by sand drifting and forming a hill, had a particular significance this time. I felt as though I was falling from a life of familiarity and security. It was my hope that my fall would have the same result of building something new, much like the sand blowing and falling over those mountaintops.

Stopping only to gas up and take a bathroom break, we made decent time, considering we were driving a truck and towing a car. We arrived at the house around lunchtime. I was willing to wait until the next day to unpack, but Jesse wanted to get all the business out of the way so we could relax. I was surprised how quickly we unloaded the truck. We even returned it to the rental agency that afternoon.

After showering, I made two cranberry and vodkas, and we sat out on the back patio. I had done a lot of landscaping with desert plants, but the yard was in need of serious care, as I wasn't able to do much on my occasional weekend trips from LA. It was my goal to make it a place that I wouldn't want to leave and where I would feel safe and secure. I knew it would take time for it to feel like home. Jesse's company gave me comfort, but I knew that in several days, I would have to confront the solitude of a being single man in a new city with no friends close by.

◈   ◈   ◈

We spent the weekend chilling. I didn't feel any pressure to unpack since I wouldn't start my new job for another couple of weeks. Jesse acted more like a host than a guest. We drank and joked about silly stuff. It was a needed distraction.

Later in the evening, we went downtown to "old Las Vegas" to hang out in some of the casinos. I went off to play some video poker. Before I knew it, Jesse had a lady on either side of him.

When he saw me approaching, he jumped up and said, "DB, I've found dessert tonight." He placed one of the lady's hands on his flexed his bicep in a show of bravado, intended for my benefit as much as for hers.

I rolled my eyes and playfully said, "Listen, Mr. Player, if you go home with them, don't expect me to come looking for your ass in the morning."

"Hey, DB, you know I was juz playin'." Again he threw out that flirtatious wink and said goodbye to his disappointed girlfriends. He had a fragrance of self-confidence and dripped with sex appeal.

We walked to the end of Fremont Street and watched the laser show.

Jesse was knock-out handsome. He was born of a biracial marriage, his mother Hispanic and his father African American. His muscular body was well concealed under the baggy clothes he wore. His voice was deep, and he had an unusual accent, a combination of street-smart arrogance and the smoothness of a seductive lover. For all the things that Jesse was doing right in the last few years, there was one aspect of his personality that would occasionally lead him astray and get him into trouble: he had a tremendous sex drive. Kevin used to tell me that even though Jesse was married, it was well known at work that he played around with a lot of the women. Granted, Jesse was entirely too sexy a man to go unnoticed by women—or men, for that matter. Apparently, he also had a reputation crediting him with an unusually large and effective piece of equipment.

After stopping in one of the coffee shops for a sandwich and some coffee, we headed back home.

I heated up the Jacuzzi. We were both pretty drunk but not ready to go to bed.

Watching the steam swirl around him, I asked, "Hey, J-Bones, you doing okay?" That was what he often called himself. I had no idea of the origin of the nickname, but it sounded "street cool" to me anyway.

He lifted the glass to his mouth. The paws prints on his tribal armband tattoo moved as his arm flexed.

"Couldn't be better, man." He dunked himself under the water then laid his head back and spread his arms across the deck of the Jacuzzi. His thick black hair, trimmed short, glistened from the water. He sported a patch under his chin and his face was framed by a day's worth of growth.

"I like your tats, Jesse. You had 'em long?" I asked, unable to take my eyes off his muscular arms.

Pointing to his arm band, he said, "This one's about five years old. The one on my shoulder has the initials of a buddy I made a childhood blood bond with." It was faded and hard to see. He leaned close to me so I could see the faded initials. Underwater, his legs rubbed against me.

Jesse was very talkative that evening and seemed to open up more than he had before.

He was proud of his popularity as an exotic dancer and an escort and recounted some of the escapades at the strip club.

"DB, I did some things I'm not real proud of back then, but ya know, it was a hot time." He boasted.

He took a long sip from his drink and continued. "Man, one time these three ladies rented one of the private rooms and asked me to dance for them. Damn, I had sex with each one of 'em that night until their money ran out."

Giving himself a little squeeze in the private parts he said, "Those ladies would tell me how they wished their husbands had the package I have."

We both sat up on the edge of the pool deck to cool off. The water ran down his smooth caramel colored skin.

It was evident from the bulge that filled my shorts that the visual I constructed about these adventures turned me on.

Jesse noticed and raised his bushy eyebrows and sported a slight grin of approval.

From out of the blue Jesse said, "You know, you're a very good looking guy, DB. Don't know how you stay in such good shape with everything you got goin' on."

Without any hesitation, he looked directly into my eyes and added, "Course, I'm not into other dudes, but if I was I'm sure it would be someone like you. You got your act together, man."

I thought, *Is Jesse hitting on me? Is this an invitation?*

Letting the alcohol speak for me I responded jokingly, "Well, man, you're my type, so you better watch out!"

A broad smile filled Jesse's face. "Well, next time we go out, we'll try to catch someone for you."

"That's a deal, man," I replied, wondering if this conversation was really happening.

Given his time spent in prison and his frequent reference to one of his gay friends, I still wondered if he had experimented on the "other side." Nevertheless, his sexuality and prowess was such an intense part of his being that I imagined he got satisfaction from awakening desires in a woman or a man. Perhaps a few more drinks that evening would have led me to see just how far Jesse would have taken his flirting game.

We were both done in from the booze and Jacuzzi. "Hey, Jesse, I think we're prunes now. How about heading in?" I got up and wrapped a towel around my waist.

Jesse jumped out quickly. I looked back. I hadn't noticed but he had taken off his swim trunks in the Jacuzzi. His back was facing towards me and the dim patio light reflected off of his wet body. He loosely wrapped a towel around himself. Still dripping wet, he came up and hung his arm around me.

Putting his mouth right next to my ear he said, "Thanks, DB. I'm havin' a great time. I hope you were able to chill a bit too." I could feel his warmth breath.

We went inside the house and I grabbed a case of beer out of the kitchen cabinet.

Jesse looked at me intently and remarked, "Big guns you got, DB. I'm trying to get my six-pack back." He rubbed his hand on his still-wet stomach. "We should work out together sometime."

Having a hard time taking my eyes off his stomach I said, "Sure, that would be cool."

I slowly walked away, as I knew my willpower was weakening. Jesse seemed to like being close to me, much closer than the physical space usually considered acceptable in Western culture—and especially among Western men. I thought of touching him at one point, but I didn't need complications right now. I didn't know how he would react. I figured—or, rather, hoped—that if it was meant to be there might be another time.

I said my good night and headed to the bedroom. He did as well.

We spent the next day doing nothing, as we worked hard the previous day unloading the truck. Jesse wanted to cook me breakfast. I thought, *Man, here's a straight guy cooking me breakfast, something most of my boyfriends never did.* After breakfast, we changed into our swim trunks, made two strong screwdrivers, and headed out to the pool.

I recall that first afternoon sitting by the pool, looking at the mountains in the distance. There was a haunting emptiness about them. Perhaps their cool hues of purple and gray were reflections of my own spirit in search of warmth. I felt like a visitor.

I must have been staring off for a few minutes. Jesse noticed and interrupted. "Ya okay, DB? Want another drink? Ya hungry?"

"I'm fine. Just daydreaming, I guess." I chuckled. Jesse was making every attempt to make me feel better.

I joked with him. "You're sounding like a waiter, and you're hired. Sure, I'll take another drink. What's on the menu, chef?"

Sporting a mischievous grin, he responded, "First, just so ya know, man, my rates are pretty steep." My mind jumped to the gutter, of course. He sure knew how to hustle and tease. "Just gonna grill the chicken and hot links and make a quick salad. Sound okay?"

"Perfect," I replied. Had it been another situation with anyone else, I would have suggested I pay the steep rates before dinner.

We had a great dinner. We finished off a second bottle of wine and lay out on the lounges watching the sunset. The peaceful atmosphere of dining outside on a beautiful desert evening brought a wave of sadness over me. I thought I should have been sharing this with my partner. Still, I was glad I wasn't alone. There were probably only three people I would have wanted to guide me through the reentry that weekend: Jesse, Angelo, or Daphne. Angelo was out of the country and wasn't able to change his schedule. Daphne would have been great company, but I needed muscle to help me with the move. I was so grateful that Jesse was not only willing but seemed honored to help me resettle. He looked up to me and appreciated that I still wanted to be friends. He once said that he never had a male figure to look up to. He felt many people had little respect for him and treated him as inferior because of his lack of education and his hourly job driving a shuttle bus. Social status was never a criterion I used when making friends. In fact, I was usually suspect of the guys anxious to climb the social ladder. I learned that lesson early on after one of my first boyfriends parted ways after growing frustrated that I didn't share the ambitious goals of joining LA's inner circle of gay society. I discovered then that I wasn't at all interested in calling those people my friends.

We both dozed off on the lounges. I was awakened by a sudden breeze the swept through the yard. I looked over, and Jesse was still knocked out. I debated whether to wake him up, thinking he'd be more comfortable in bed, especially if the evening turned cool. I woke him up and coaxed him to his room. He crashed on top of the bed. I stood there for a moment and looked at him. For some reason,

I was overcome with emotion, and my eyes filled with tears. I was grateful for his help and friendship, but still lonely for the one that I had expected to be with me for a lifetime.

Jesse left after the weekend was over. I drove him to the airport so he could catch the short flight back to LA.

Giving me a long-lasting hug, Jesse said, "Thanks again, DB. I hope you invite me back again soon." I could feel his strong hands rub my back.

Without hesitation, I replied, "Hey, man, you're always welcome to visit. I'd like that."

Jesse gave me a quick squeeze on my arm and walked away, turning around once to wave to me.

I glanced around and noticed that our farewell had caught the attention of the other passengers waiting to check in. *What the hell,* I thought. It felt good to be acknowledged this way by another man, even though I knew he was returning to his family.

I drove back home, opened the gate to the driveway, and parked. The realization that I was alone in an unfamiliar place finally hit me hard. I felt the loneliness start to creep in and surround me—an awful sensation of abandonment but relief that I had made is this far. I went into the house and sobbed uncontrollably for hours.

Four:

♪♫ ♪♫ ♪♫

Connecting Past and Present

I t had only been a few days since Jesse left. I knew it would be a difficult adjustment to be alone, not to have someone complete my sentences, and to know that the day would lack the familiarity of routine.

I appreciated all the help Jesse had given me but I wished my best friend Angelo had been there to spend the first few days with me. I always joked that Angelo was the Lucy to my Ethel, although he would claim it was the other way around. We had known one another since attending the same Catholic high school in Chicago. Of all my dear friends, he was the one person who I could call in the middle of the night to talk. We shared everything. If I was to make it through this transition, I knew I would need his support.

Our lives had been strangely intertwined since high school. We went off to college in different states, him to the music conservatory at Northwestern University in Chicago, and me to the University of Wisconsin. Angelo was something of a prodigy when it came to music. He took up the guitar when he was very young. In high school, he was selected to join the prestigious Monterey All-American High School Jazz Band, part of the annual Monterey (California) Jazz Festival's musician development project. He toured around the world one summer and subsequently received a full scholarship to the conservatory at Northwestern. At first his father wasn't keen on him pursuing a career in music. He would speak of his brother— Angelo's uncle—Niccolo, who had been an accomplished bass guitar player back in the day but died at a relatively young age, succumbing to a lifestyle punctuated by late nights, drugs, and constant travel. Angelo's father wanted more for his son. Everyone figured that Angelo must have inherited his talent from his uncle Nick. The full college scholarship quickly changed his father's mind, and he soon became an ardent supporter of Angelo's musical career.

Angelo got married while at the conservatory. He would later admit it was a mistake, that he and his wife were young and stupid. After a year it ended in divorce. Her parents were from the affluent North Shore of Chicago, and they didn't think a musician was a good enough mate for their daughter. Angelo came out a year later. After graduation, Angelo stayed in Chicago to get some street cred honing his bass guitar skills with various local jazz and blues bands.

I came out in my senior year. After graduation, I returned to Chicago a more confident and secure young man. I ended up finding a job as a bank auditor, far from what an idealistic college graduate had hoped to be doing. The economy at the time was not a friend to inexperienced job hunters, and there seemed to be more opportunities for musicians than business graduates.

Angelo and I resumed our friendship. A fan of jazz and blues, I used to hang out in some of the clubs on the weekends. I'd find out where Angelo was performing and listen to him play. He seemed to enjoy having me in the audience. We would end up having drinks after the show, and it didn't take long for us to acknowledge to one another that we were gay. Our bodies had matured from boyish to manly since our high school days, and we found one another attractive. We dated frequently during that year after graduation. Angelo was a poster child for the Italian stud. He grew up in an Italian neighborhood on the West Side of Chicago. He had a swagger that defined his status as eldest son in a traditional Italian family. Where some guys put on a swagger to impress, for Angelo it came naturally. He was confident and fully aware of how handsome he was yet was humble and always approachable. He'd often take me to his family's home for dinner on weekends. We both were grateful for having grown up in ethnic and culturally robust neighborhoods. We were of the last generation to be raised in well-defined ethnic neighborhoods where during a simple walk to school you could be overwhelmed by the smell of Czech sauerkraut and pastries or the marinara sauce and pasta of Little Italy. The boundaries of those neighborhoods began to dissolve years ago. Of course, along with the fond traditions we remembered, narrow-minded and prejudiced behaviors incubated in those insulated communities. His mom was an outspoken yet affectionate woman. She treated me like another son. She always thought I was younger than Angelo even though our birthdays were only one month apart, and she called me *bambino*. When Angelo felt playful, he'd call me Bam. As we got older he shortened it to Bo, taken from Svoboda, which most folks found hard to pronounce, let alone spell. Occasionally, I would call him Nico, the childhood nickname anointed him by his family. It was short for his middle name, Niccolo.

His father was muscular and dark skinned, with thick, wavy black hair and a heavy beard. He was always wearing a wife beater, exposing his hairy chest and strong shoulders. He worked construction for the county and demonstrated hardiness typical of many first- and second-generation immigrants. His English was broken. Angelo was always trying to correct him, which made him angry and usually led to a short but intense argument in Italian.

Angelo inherited all the good qualities of his father: strength, dark olive skin, small swirls of black hair, and curls of body hair that seemed to be deliberately placed to accent his chest, stomach, and legs. His hands were a bittersweet juxtaposition of rugged and strong and well-manicured. He kept his mustache well-trimmed. What I remembered most, though, was the fresh yet musky smell when I was near him. Nature had clearly endowed him an intoxicating cocktail of manly sexuality, good looks, and a disarming personality.

Angelo was the most sensual and erotic man I had ever been with. His sleepy eyes invited, his deep gravelly voice incited, and his handsome and beautiful body delighted. Yes, it was a steamy affair. Before we made love he would whisper in Italian, *"Bello, ti desidero,"* which roughly translates to "Handsome, I want you." When he held me in his strong arms and whispered to me in Italian, I surrendered completely.

He always wore a gold ring with a single row of small diamonds, the one in the center larger than the others. I'd never forget the first night we met. He left the ring on my nightstand and forgot to put it on the next morning. He later told me he did it on purpose to have an excuse to come back. To this day, seeing him with that ring brings a smile to my face. Occasionally, I'd kid him and say, "Careful where you leave that ring now." He'd just grin and slap me on the rear.

At the time, we both instinctively felt we were meant to be long-lasting friends, not lovers. We both were young and busy, perhaps foolishly so, and not able to appreciate the feelings we had for one another. We had diverse career goals. He started traveling to other cities with a local jazz band. His good looks and seductive personality only added to his popularity as a musician. When he did his bass guitar solos, the crowds would stand and scream their approval. We grew very close that year in Chicago, probably closer than we realized at the time. Angelo and I never discussed trying to stay near one another though we remained close friends. We were always honest and didn't keep secrets from one another, but perhaps the exception was the deep feelings that we shared and suppressed for so many years.

After one year in Chicago, I got frustrated with my auditing job. I was, after all, an idealistic college graduate looking for a job that would inspire me. I really wanted to do something with my degrees in botany and business. It was an odd combination, but I figured I would eventually find something that excited me.

I relocated to Los Angeles for the job with the State of California, enthusiastic about moving to the West Coast and finding a job that seemed ideally suited for my training and interests. As Angelo's career took off, he would frequently call me when he had a gig near Los Angeles. We'd get together whenever possible and talk routinely on the phone. As best friends we shared our joys and successes and offered support for one another when we needed a shoulder to cry on. We always respected our involvements with other people. In time, when we would reconnect, we'd often sleep together for companionship without sex. It often struck me as odd that I'd be in bed with this hot Italian and, feeling his body next to me, I'd experience the longer-lasting sensations of security, warmth, and love, rather than the brief gratification received from a sexual encounter.

All my boyfriends and lovers knew of the tight friendship we had. Even thought I was always loyal to my partners, it was a prerequisite they accepted the relationship that Angelo and I shared. He was like a brother, a friend, a confidant. Losing Angelo would've been the most devastating loss imaginable, next to that of a partner. I had recovered from a lot of things, but I didn't know what I'd do without him in my life.

Given Angelo's nomadic lifestyle, he was fortunate to avoid the trap of drugs that ended the careers of many of his contemporaries and his uncle Niccolo. The worst he succumbed to was a fondness for weed, which we both shared in moderation. On the road much of the time, he was never able to sustain anything resembling a relationship. Despite the seemingly glamorous lifestyle, the life of a musician had its downside. Angelo still lacked love and companionship. While he met many people outside of the music business, he never was able to support a long term relationship. He complained of always being the bridesmaid and never the bride.

❖   ❖   ❖

Another good friend, Daphne, was on her way back from a trip back to LA after visiting family in Chicago. She left me a message, saying that she wanted to stop in Las Vegas to see me. She thought she could help me get settled and unpacked. We hadn't seen one another since the funeral. If it was anyone other than her or Angelo, I would have turned down the offer, as I was feeling depressed and wasn't sure I was in the mood for company. I sent her a text, saying that it would be nice to see a familiar face. As nice as my house was, it still didn't feel like home.

Angelo met Daphne after about five years on the road with various bands. When he formed his own jazz/blues band called UnderFunk, he needed an attorney to handle contracts. A colleague had introduced him to Daphne, a Chicago attorney who had done considerable legal work for other music groups. She was several years older than Angelo. A very attractive woman in her early forties, Daphne was very articulate and outspoken. Rather tall and full-figured, she usually let her beautiful long red hair drift past her shoulders. She dressed immaculately. While attractive, Daphne had been the victim of domestic violence in a previous marriage. It left her emotionally damaged and reluctant to become seriously involved again with a man. She and Angelo became good friends, as he was non-threatening to her as a gay man and they enjoyed one another's company. Soon after Daphne got involved with Angelo's group, she was offered a great position with a law firm in San Diego. She jumped at the chance to get out to the West Coast but continued doing legal work for Angelo.

He introduced us, thinking we would connect with one another. We found we had a lot in common. She was an alumna of the same university, we both loved jazz and blues, and we shared the same political views. Daphne had also had spent time in the Peace Corps in Sierra Leon when she was younger. I was intrigued by her stories of living abroad. Whenever possible, we would take a quick road trip to another city and catch one of Angelo's shows. In time, the three of us started doing a lot together whenever time permitted. When Angelo was in Southern California, the three of us would get together for dinner. Daphne had a small cottage on Lake Michigan about an hour away from Chicago, just across the border in Indiana. Some of my favorite memories were of the weekends in the fall when the three of us would fly back to the Midwest and gather there for a long weekend retreat.

Daphne spent three days with me. She helped me organize the kitchen and my office. She was a wizard when it came to hooking up electronics like DVD players, stereo components, and computers.

We talked and laughed a lot, just the medicine I needed. During one of our marathon talk sessions one evening, she asked me if I thought I would ever want to have another boyfriend.

"Daph, for sure I'm not looking for a relationship right now. I need time to clear my head. I just don't know if I'm capable of loving anyone again." I suddenly felt sad.

"Of course you are," Daphne countered rather forcefully. "I know you, Wes. You're not a loner. You have a need to share your life with someone. You do need a break right now, but don't rule it out."

Daphne brushed her long red hair back and continued. "The day will come when you'll be ready again. You're a good catch for someone too, so you have to be careful of someone taking advantage of you. I think you're a bit vulnerable right now."

"Thanks, Dr. Daphne. You should have a TV show!" We both laughed. I know she was trying to be protective of me, even though another relationship was the furthest thing from my mind.

I purposely changed the subject. "Have you talked to Angelo lately?"

"Not since the funeral. He left town soon afterward for a series of appearances in New York as part of an annual jazz caravan held by a half dozen or so jazz clubs in the city, then on to a European tour with his new group, UnderFunk. That boy keeps busy." She shook her head.

"Yeah, I'm happy for him, Daph, but I don't get to see him as often as I'd like to, especially now. We talk and text a lot, but it's not the same."

Noticing that I was disingenuous in my enthusiasm for his tour, Daphne added, "Well, every time I talk with him, he asks about you, Wes. You know it broke his heart to see you at the funeral. He knew you were keeping a lot inside."

"Really?" I asked. My pleasure in hearing this must have been evident. Daphne gave me an encouraging smile. "Well, I'll be okay. I always have been. Hopefully, everyone will be able to come here for the annual dinner in a couple of months. It'll give me something to look forward to."

Daphne gave me a hug. She said, "You can count on it. Angelo already told me he'll be here."

I was glad to hear her say that.

When it was time for Daphne to leave, I realized how much help she had been, not only to unpack and organize the house, but also to replenish some of the strength and confidence I would need to move forward.

PART II:
PLANNED SERENDIPITY

Five:

⁊⁊· ⁊⁊· ⁊⁊·

Settling In—Friends, Some Benefits

The first three months in Las Vegas were like a bungee jump of emotions. At one moment, plunges would find me depressed and crying, the sunlight blinding and the nighttime suffocating, and the next moment I would bounce back with self-control and renewed optimism about the future. I learned that my once strong and resilient character could be vulnerable and fragile. For the first time in my life, my personal compass was unable to point me toward any specific direction. I struggled to adopt the "take things as they come" attitude that I had committed myself to following.

I found myself waking up before dawn, sitting outside in the dark and sipping my coffee, waiting for the first light of the morning. As the first rays of the sun frosted the nearby mountains with their signature pink haze, their towering presence reminded me I was in a place yet unfamiliar and foreign. I spent those hours thinking about my life, talking to myself, and debating whether the move to Las Vegas had been the right thing to do. Long after I became settled the early morning coffee klatches with myself had become routine.

While I missed my friends in LA, the small city atmosphere of Las Vegas was starting to grow on me. I was fortunate that my new job with the BLM was going well. Being able to get out of the office on occasion and visit land holdings in the desert made it enjoyable and offered a distraction from my lack of social life. Not knowing how long I would call Las Vegas my home, my only objective socially was to cultivate a couple of new friendships. I no longer found the bars very enjoyable, and I wasn't a joiner of clubs or the best candidate for volunteer work. I knew this would make it more challenging to meet people in a new city. I had to find new ways to meet people. I was engaging in small groups but functioned best in one-on-one social situations. Not one for small talk, I loved discussing politics and current social issues. It would have been easy to turn inward and become reclusive. Occasionally, I went to movies alone, but more often I would hike into the Red Rock National Preserve and from a hilltop would sit for a couple of hours staring out over the panorama of the Las Vegas valley, daydreaming about what kind of future I would encounter.

It was my day off, but my internal clock, regulated by the sunrise, woke me up by 6:00 a.m. I loved the desert air, the dry clear skies, and the view of the mountains from nearly every window of the house. I went to the bathroom to wash up. Looking in the mirror, I saw a tired, yet still-handsome face, perhaps showing the strain of the past year and a half. I was still in good shape, despite losing about ten pounds. During the ordeal of caring for Kevin, working, and managing the household, I still managed to go to the gym, sometimes at 3:00 a.m. before work. I knew if I didn't take care of myself I would be in no condition to care of anyone else.

After months in the desert, I was already getting my color back. I was surprised how just a short time in the desert sun darkened my skin tone several shades. To some degree I inherited my father's darker complexion. I recall vividly an experience from my childhood that forever changed him and left an impression on me as well. While driving back to the Midwest from a car trip to Florida, we stopped at a motel in South Carolina. After walking to the motel office to get a room, my dad returned quickly back to the car with a stunned look on his face. We were anxious to get out of the car after a long day's drive and asked him what was wrong. He turned to my mother and said that they had no rooms for us. I didn't exactly understand what he meant at the time but the look on my Mother's face told me that it wasn't good. I later learned that my dad had met discrimination face to face for the first time because of his dark hair, strong features, and his skin color, darkened by a few days in the Florida sun. He was never the same after that experience. He subsequently sacrificed friendships as a result of his refusal to tolerate prejudicial behavior, something that earned him my respect as a man of principles.

❖   ❖   ❖

It had been a long while since I was sexually and socially active. Kevin's illness refocused my energy to that of caregiver. I successfully repressed my sexual needs most of the time. On a couple of occasions, I slipped out to a bathhouse for a quick release, but it was rarely fulfilling. My need for social contact weighed more heavily on me than the sexual desires.

I had started to explore a couple of the online dating (hookup) websites. New to me, these sites initially made me think, *Man, it should be easy to meet guys—not only for a sexual outlet, but eventually to establish some new local friendships.* I knew I wasn't receptive to owning the responsibility of another relationship right now and I navigated cautiously through the online dating waters.

I soon discovered that the online candy store was more often a shop of horrors. Initially, many of the men seemed to be attractive, at least those that had photos of their faces and not just body parts. I got suspicious when I noticed that some of the same photos would appear on the profiles of different guys. Maybe cyber dating was really more about cyber fantasies. I had come to think that many social networks seemed to offer a false sense of community and a distorted, if not perverse, view of what friends really were. You could be "flagged," "friended," or "winked" at or be sent "hugs" and "kisses." But rarely would anyone be willing to converse with you. I didn't want to be just another "notch in the crotch" of the social network evangelists competing for the number of "friends" on their profile.

Despite my lack of experience with online dating, I made several attempts to pursue some of the guys with whom I seemed to share some mutual attraction. Most of my attempts, however, didn't get past first base. Typical of these dating disasters was a bartender at a one of the strip hotels and the other a young attorney who worked for a local firm. Unfortunately, I wasn't able to make a connection with either one, sexually or as friends. The bartender brought his work home, literally. The attorney had a demeanor that reflected the obnoxious personal injury ads run by his firm on TV. I remained aloof and a bit disconnected, until I met a twenty-two-year-old named Marcus.

I privately called him my "young blood." When I logged on to a popular hookup site that evening, I wasn't looking for anyone that young. I usually screened my searches to look for guys in their mid-thirties to forties, thinking some degree of maturity would be packaged in a body that still had some hope of retaining its vigor and athletic appearance. I usually didn't respond to young guys, thinking they just wanted to be taken care of, a role that didn't interest me at all. After Marcus initiated an online conversation with me one evening, I made an exception and never regretted it. He was an athletic-looking African American man who looked older than his twenty-two years. His sleepy eyes framed by heavy eyebrows were seductive, and his slow and deliberate speech was delivered in a deep, masculine voice. His dark skin was tight and smooth, with wisps of black hair on his chest and stomach. He was smaller than me but muscular and well-proportioned in every regard. This sexy young man with a heavy beard that he sculpted into a sexy goatee and mustache made my heart race. He was warm, sweet, honest, and had a happy disposition. While I considered myself sexually versatile, Marcus's preference was to submit and be topped. I was more than happy to oblige. Neither of us made demands. He reminded me of an earlier time when I had boyfriends like him. It was an arrangement in which we both were getting what we wanted. We didn't talk politics or weather. Actually, we didn't talk much at all. We either went to a movie or played on the Wii—and of course, played games under the covers. He would always sleep over. I felt lucky to find someone who liked to cuddle all night. Perhaps he and I subconsciously agreed to use one another, him looking for a father figure, and me resurrecting youthful fantasies that had for the most part become distant memories. He was going to community college to study theater. I wasn't sure about his acting skills, but he certainly had the goods to become a successful model. The alarm would go off at 7:30 a.m. I'd have to wake him up and drop him off at school.

Sometimes Angelo would call me mid-morning and ask if "soccer mom" had dropped off his kid today, referring to Marcus. Angelo knew he would occasionally spend the night with me. We'd laugh. I'd tell him how guilty I felt. He'd reassure me that it was ok, as long as I didn't file for adoption.

While often a critic of the shallowness of social networking sites, I admit for what I was looking for, it was an efficient way to meet people. Given my state of mind, I gave in to my desires and welcomed Marcus to my bed often during the first few months. His innocence and simple, uncomplicated playfulness were an irresistible prescription for what ailed me, even though I knew it wouldn't last long. He was a very intelligent guy, but our abbreviated conversations reflected the gap of a generation and his limited life experiences. I began to fear I was getting attached to him and him to me. His age notwithstanding, I wasn't ready to get involved again. Sometimes, when he called, I gave an excuse that I was busy. I would not only feel guilty for lying to him, but would also become frustrated for not letting my physical and emotional needs get satisfied in the ways that he did so well. I continued with the routine of pizza, a movie, an evening of great sex, and waking up with him nestled in my arms, but I knew at some point I would have to push him out of the nest and set him free. He needed to experience the things that would help a young man develop self-esteem and independence. I just hoped when that time came we would remain friends.

Despite my intermittent fling with Marcus, I was feeling disconnected. I really needed someone closer to my age with whom I could relate. It was a Colombian national working on a water engineering project in the desert with whom I first felt a legitimate connection. He would best symbolize the struggle in adjusting to my new life, and the difficulties of repeating or replacing what I had lost. I knew that I had lost more than a companion when Kevin died. He symbolized the stability, security, and most of all, a focus on the future.

❖   ❖   ❖

Raul was an engineer from Colombia who had lived in the States for ten years—Chicago, to be exact. We met at a conference in Phoenix. He happened to be on a long-term assignment in Las Vegas. We connected immediately on several levels. We were nearly the same age, he had lived in my hometown for many years, and I had lived in South America and was familiar with Colombian culture. During my UN mission in Ecuador, I often traveled—

albeit with difficulty—across the border into Colombia. As it turned out, a former UN colleague lived in his hometown of Medellin. It was probably this connection that brought us close together rather quickly. I know he appreciated meeting someone bilingual and, in particular, someone who understood and was interested in his Hispanic heritage.

Perhaps because of his light complexion, he did not immediately give away his ethnic background. While his native Spanish gave him command and authority, his English, while good for a second language, carried a strong accent. It made him more innocent and vulnerable. I found these two dimensions of Raul attractive and disarming. We both used language as a way to signal our respective moods. His seductive personality would emerge when he spoke in his Colombian Spanish, which was deep and articulate. When he wanted to be in control, which also telegraphed sexual interest, he would speak in his commanding native tongue. Sometimes when I wanted to start some mischief I would initiate the conversation in Spanish. He quickly caught on to that little trick. It ultimately became our secret code. Once, at a small party, Raul, who naturally would speak in English as a courtesy to the hosts and guests, pulled me aside and whispered to me in Spanish, "Listo, hombre?" I responded with a broad smile. Even in a Spanish whisper I knew what was on his mind.

Where I was cautious and intentionally regulated my feelings, he was more impulsive and became emotionally involved very quickly. Raul recognized that I was still resistant to becoming seriously involved, but he would encourage me just to let things happen. "If it changes you, let it," he would say. I had made some significant changes in my life, but they were anything but impulsive. The move to California from Chicago and the UN mission in South America were researched and planned. This time was different. I knew I needed to shake things up.

I spent more time with Raul than with anyone else. We dated continuously for almost a month. My fluency in Spanish and love of South America created a natural bond. Being with him was another way of reconnecting with Hispanic culture. My earlier experience in Ecuador with the UN gave me a great appreciation for the richness and variety of cultures in our southern hemisphere. It's a shame that so many people don't realize that "south of the border" encompasses not a single Hispanic culture but many unique countries where even the Spanish language is different within their respective borders.

On one memorable afternoon when we both had the same day off, we packed up a lunch and drove out into the desert, about a half hour outside of Las Vegas. It was a beautiful day. The clear, dry desert air was refreshing, and it was early enough in the year that the severe heat had not yet set in. Some of the yuccas and early blooming cacti were displaying beautiful florescence. I was pleased that Raul appreciated the same things. We hiked up a familiar trail that I had taken several times. After a half hour, we started to near the base of the mountains. We stopped for a second and could hear the sound of rushing water. The spring snowmelt in the mountains had begun, and a normally dry creek bed was full and moving swiftly. Not many people walked this trail. I considered it a well-kept secret and was always reluctant to tell anyone exactly where it was.

I grabbed Raul's hand. It was thick and work worn. As we hiked in a little further, there was a side path veering off the main trail.

"Raul, I have a surprise for you." I pulled him off the main trail on to a small path leading through some tall brush.

"Where are you taking me, Beto? They would never find me out here." It was difficult for him to pronounce "Wes" since there was no "W" in the Spanish alphabet, so he decided to call me Beto, which was short for my middle name, Roberto.

"That's the whole point. Once I have my way with you, I can hide the evidence, and no one will ever know." I gave him a mischievous wink.

Raul gestured as though he was a prisoner with his hands tied together. "I promise I will be a cooperative prisoner." His round, unshaven face that sported added to the fantasy.

He liked my suggestive talk. I was waiting for him to start talking in Spanish. Then I'd know for sure that I was the one in trouble.

In a few short minutes the sound of splashing water grew louder. We made our way through some brush and then around a stand of desert willows. Finally, we arrived at the prize. It couldn't have been a more beautiful and private spot. An eight foot waterfall cascaded over boulders into a pool the size of a small swimming pool. The water was exceptionally clear and ice cold, having made its way from the frigid high altitudes where the snowpack was still substantial.

"You're always full of surprises. This is spectacular." Raul was clearly impressed, and didn't hesitate to hug me and give me a big kiss. "How did you ever find this? The trail isn't even marked."

"This area is under consideration by the BLM for preservation status, and they brought me here awhile back to see it first-hand. Nice, isn't it?"

Raul replied, "It's perfect, Beto." Taking off his sweatshirt, he revealed his broad chest, which suited his short and stocky physique.

Although Raul was very handsome, his body type would normally not have captured my attention. It was his deep voice, seductive eyes, and self-confidence that drew me to him.

I watched as he rushed to unpack the *medianoches*, or sandwiches, we had bought at a Cuban market. He was clearly excited to be with me that day. I opened up the wine, and we made business of our picnic lunch.

I had barely finished my first glass of wine when Raul, with a flirtatious look on his face, commanded in Spanish, "Beto, come sit next to me." As he moved to embrace me the veins seemed to dance along his thick and muscular forearms.

I naturally obeyed. We embraced and kissed. At first I was a bit self-conscious. After all, this was a site for which I'd be working on a business plan. But I soon disposed of that thought and surrendered to my aroused senses and Raul's influence.

As the warmth of the afternoon enveloped our shady paradise, Raul removed his shirt, exposing a dark mark on his shoulder.

Putting my hand on his shoulder I asked, "Raul, is that a tattoo?"

Surprised that I had noticed, Raul replied, "Not anymore. I had one when I was a teenager but had it removed when I moved to the United States."

Raul, seeming anxious to change the subject, leaned over and started to kiss me and get playful. The waterfall and pool made it tempting to strip down and get into some serious sexual play. It seemed so natural, unlike the sex many men have in parks or other public places, but Raul sensed my uneasiness about getting too wild at a place where I could have to return for work.

Raul's smile suddenly disappeared, and his expression grew more serious. He tilted his head to the side. "Beto, I think I'm falling in love with you." He was still holding me tightly. "You are so special to me." Little beads of sweat formed on his shaved head.

I didn't know what to say at first. I cared for Raul deeply, but love was an emotion that was difficult for me absorb. I hadn't expected to meet someone so soon, especially someone so willing to get seriously involved.

Not taking time to think through my response, I said, "I love you too, Raul." He noticed right away that I avoided the words "in love." His English was proficient enough to understand the nuance.

Before I could say anything he stroked my face, and said, "That's okay, Beto. I don't expect you to be at the same place as me just yet. I just want you to know how I feel toward you. I only hope that someday you will feel the same."

I was so relieved and a little embarrassed at the same time, but Raul immediately made me realize there was no pressure. I couldn't help but wonder if I would ever be able to feel the way he did.

We spent another hour by the waterfall and pool, saying little, holding one another. We watched the water pour into the pool, swirl and bubble, and then move on down the stream. The bubbles passed and slowly disappeared, similar to people in our lives. I thought, *Friends meet, they are with us for a while, and then they move on.* It was somewhat of a spiritual moment for me. I wasn't a religious person, but in a strange way I felt that the universe was somehow registering satisfaction in the direction my life was heading.

We packed up and headed back to the car. During the trip home, we didn't say much more. He kept his hand on my leg while I drove back to Las Vegas. I dropped him off at his apartment. He had a meeting early the next day, as did I. We gave each other a kiss and said goodnight.

Although I felt a growing attachment to Raul, we were only able to get together every couple of weeks because of our respective schedules. He traveled often, and my BLM work was becoming increasingly demanding, especially as the company started to see the positive impact I was having.

I had moved to Las Vegas with the notion that over time I might meet one or two guys with whom I could develop a great friendship, if not some side benefits. The emptiness of this "strategy" had become apparent. Denying myself the pursuit of natural feelings and establishing strict boundaries that I wouldn't cross only prolonged the necessary adjustment and recalibration that I needed in order to heal and move forward. With the speed of life as it was, it seemed only natural to want to make a personal connection with someone who could help make the short journey fulfilling and worthwhile.

Over the weeks, I started to let down my guard and become more open to the idea that maybe Raul offered me the new, alternative start. Little did I know at the time we started communicating on the Internet that he would play a major role in my "resettlement" experience and shake up my world in ways I never would have anticipated.

Six:

⑃⑃ ⑃⑃ ⑃⑃

Anxiety in the Andes

The job at BLM was going well. I enjoyed the work and especially the opportunity to be outdoors at some of the sites planned for preservation. I didn't mind the long days. In fact, it kept my mind occupied. I only saw Raul occasionally. He was busy with work as well. We tried to make sure no more than two weeks passed without seeing one another.

It was early on a Saturday morning and I had just dropped Marcus off for a morning class after one of our evening sessions. My cell phone started to ring. It wasn't the familiar ring tone I used for friends. It was an unknown caller. I was hesitant to answer so I let the voice mail pick up. Afterwards I thought the maybe Angelo was traveling again and used a hotel phone to check on me.

I listened to the message, expecting Angelo's deep voice to groan, "hey, fella." But I was surprised, as the voice was distant, distressed, and in Spanish. The message was short. "Wes, llámame de pronto. Necesito ayuda ...en serio. Tico." It was Tico, a friend I had met while working in Quito, Ecuador, ten years ago. It was unusual for him to sound distressed. He was always upbeat, even in situations where normal people would be in a state of panic and frenzy. I knew I needed to take a deep breath before I returned the call. It was ironic that my new friend, Raul, from Colombia, and my buddy Tico in Ecuador, places so far away, would ultimately have such a huge impact on me. I made a quick drink, a screwdriver with a splash of cranberry juice. After all, it was after 11 a.m.

Tico and I had stayed in touch all those years. I visited Quito twice since I left Ecuador, and he had come to LA to visit as well. His Costa Rican–born parents named him Tico, after the nickname that Costa Ricans used to describe themselves.

I had just reported to duty as a UN advisor in Ecuador when I met him. It was my first overseas work experience, and I was both excited and terrified. I learned Spanish while in Spain for my junior year abroad but took a crash refresher course just before leaving for Quito. I accepted the mission in Ecuador in part because I had been there once before as a tourist and also because for all the third world countries in South and Central America, Ecuador had become a model for U.S.-style democracy and was a friendly ally of the United States. My experience there gave me a true sense of what it meant to be alone and on your own. It allowed me to develop a keen appreciation for other cultures, and it gifted me with friendships that would impact my life in ways I couldn't have imagined.

I recalled it was his smile I first remembered when I got off the plane after an all-night flight from Los Angeles nearly a decade ago.

❖   ❖   ❖

My mind flashed back to some of the memories of that year in Ecuador.

The flight from LA was not without drama. After what seemed like hours of turbulence from tropical storms, we were diverted to land in Guayaquil, the second-largest city in Ecuador, located on the Pacific coast. Quito, the capital, was located at an altitude of nearly ten thousand feet in the middle of the cordillera of the Andes. Landing on a good day was always something of a challenge, but during bad weather, it was a crapshoot. Many Ecuadorian presidents never saw reelection because of fatal air crashes. I was partially relieved to have been diverted, but I had already been up twenty hours, and my appearance was beginning to look less than sterling. I was hoping that once I got to Quito, I could go directly to my hotel room, shower, and contemplate the adventure I was about embark on for the next year.

Upon learning that the Quito weather had improved, we boarded the plane and headed off to the colonial capital. After the hour-long flight, we began our descent into Quito. I tried to make myself look presentable but could feel that what had been five o'clock shadow was now more like a 10:00 or 11:00 p.m. shadow. With the help of the wrinkled clothes I had been wearing for nearly thirty hours, I imagined that I looked like someone who had slept in a cardboard box all night.

The landing was uneventful, my first "thank you, universe" moment. As the plane taxied toward the modest terminal, I saw a small group of people huddled together on the tarmac. There were no fancy gateways connected to the terminal for deplaning. It was the old-fashioned stairway and walk to the terminal, subjecting you to whatever elements with which Mother Nature had decided to embellish the day. I grabbed my jacket and carry-on and descended the stairs, inhaling for the first time that rarified air I had been warned about and experienced on previous high-altitude travels. Because of the altitude, it seemed as if the clouds were within arms' reach, and looking towards the horizon, I could see the snowy tops of several volcanoes. It was a beautiful and almost surreal moment. As I neared the bottom of the stairs, I again noticed the small group of three men standing about fifty feet away. I figured they were waiting for relatives on the same flight. As I began to walk past them, one of them yelled out, "Senor Wesley!" I barely recognized what he was saying, given the noise of the still-whirring jets. The youngest gentleman of the group stepped up and introduced himself as Tico Ayala. He was carrying a photo of me so they could identify me. He welcomed me to Quito, addressing me in Spanish but pronouncing my name in English with almost no accent. At that moment, two things flashed in my mind: People were speaking Spanish as their first language, and I wasn't an accidental tourist traveling in anonymity.

Tico was a local reporter for the Quito newspaper, *El Diario*. He had a boyish appearance. He was short and slight of build. His jet black hair framed a broad smile punctuated by white teeth that seemed to reflect the bright equatorial sunlight. Accompanying him was a photographer who was clicking away as we spoke. An older man introduced himself as an assistant from the local UN office and explained that he would be my contact for relocation assistance.

Tico was very gracious and had a twinkle in his eye. My "gaydar," though dulled from the trip, intercepted a nonverbal transmission that transcended cultural and linguistic boundaries. He briefly explained that he was asked to cover my arrival, which apparently was considered newsworthy in this Andean capital city. I was both flattered and horrified. Could my one famous photo op have occurred at a worse time? After a short interview on the way to customs and baggage claim, we posed for a couple of photos in front of the tie-dye-painted Ecuatoriana jetliner. The UN courier had arranged for a taxi to take to me to the Hotel Intercontinental, where I had stayed years earlier as a tourist. Before Tico retreated with the group, he managed to hand me a business card, which I figured was a standard card with contact information from the newspaper. I stuffed it in my passport folder. Shortly afterward, a taxi pulled up, and an airport employee walked up to me with my bag in hand. I felt like an honored guest.

After checking in to the hotel, I showered and went down to the coffee shop to have a quick bite before it closed. I was starving and a bit dizzy from the altitude. I had been forewarned that it would take several weeks to completely adapt. Light meals with a bit of alcohol after each was the recommended way to transition from the lowlands. While sipping on a cocktail, I pulled out the card that Tico gave me at the airport. Expecting to see the newspaper logo and contact information, I was surprised to see a blank card with a short handwritten note: "Tico Ayala, Se Alquila Apartamentos—Quito." I thought, *Here was an enterprising young guy, renting apartments as well as working for the newspaper.* I figured it wouldn't hurt to give him a call.

The UN office had provided me a list of housing options as part of my relocation packet, but they were concentrated mainly in the "colony," an area of Quito where most of the foreigners lived. From the beginning, I had decided that I wanted to immerse myself in the Ecuadorian culture, not spend my time here isolated with nonnatives and insulated from the local customs and culture. Time would prove this to have been a challenging, but not a regrettable, decision. While I survived my Quito experience with many great memories, there were many times I would have clicked my heels to get back to an LA grocery store to buy peanut butter and a can of real ground coffee. As a coffee addict, I had great anticipation of living in one of the fertile coffee-growing regions of the world. The great irony was that Ecuador exported its entire coffee production. I was shocked to learn that all the locals drank instant Nescafé. *What a cruel welcome,* I thought, *for a coffee lover like myself.* This situation was quickly remedied with shipments of coffee from friends in the States.

The UN covered the first four weeks of hotel expenses, but I was eager to settle into my own quarters. I called Tico after several days, and we agreed to meet one Saturday to look for an apartment. After several days of looking around and learning the local idiomatic apartment-rent-speak, we found a little penthouse on the top of an eight-story apartment building on Calle Amazonas, about a two-kilometer walk from the old colonial section where my office was located. Calle Amazonas was in the "newer" part of Quito, the Mariscal District, a younger, more hip area with shops, cafés, and a movie theater. The apartment was furnished, with two bedrooms, a large, open living room, and a wrap-around balcony on two sides. It looked out over the slumbering Pichincha volcano that towered over the city. The volcano erupted violently four years after I left and covered that part of the city in ash. Considered high-end for the average Quito resident, the apartment was cheap by U.S. standards. My place would eventually become "headquarters" for the small group of gay friends I would make while living there.

It was only a twenty-minute walk to my office. What would normally have been an easy walk for me, the ten-thousand-foot altitude had me arriving to work huffing and puffing the first couple of weeks. Once I became acclimated, I looked forward to the jaunt. Lacking a car, I found I had started to relax and acquired a slower pace that matched the local Quiteños. I fell into a routine of stopping at a small bar about halfway home for a beer and ceviche. The owner, an older lady who appeared to be of Indian descent, soon acknowledged me as a regular, and I didn't have to order. She had a young lady bring my beer and ceviche to the table before I had a chance to take off my jacket.

I had been in Quito just short of two weeks and was walking back from work when I heard someone call out at me.

"Hola, Senor Wes!" exclaimed a voice from behind me.

Not having had made any friends at this point, I was a bit surprised to hear my name called. When I turned around, I was confronted by a big toothy smile and those sleepy eyes, which at the airport seemed innocent but now carried a sexier message. Tico was decked out in a tight T-shirt and even tighter jeans. It was the style in the capital. He was much more relaxed than when I saw him at the airport or when we were looking for apartments. I told him I'd called to let him know how happy I was with the apartment, but I wasn't able to get through. He apologized and said he had a fight with his roommate and had to get his own apartment. That confirmed my original thought. I guess gay men were everywhere. Without saying anything, we both seemed to acknowledge one another's "secret."

Tico seemed relaxed, happy, and eager to get to know me. He quickly invited me to go with him for a drink. He walked me two blocks down a side street that I hadn't yet explored. We entered a building with no exterior marking except a small front window that was covered in white miniature lights. We walked in the door. It was a small, dark place. The bar was right by the door. There were about eight stools. Further back were four small tables with two or three chairs at each table. That was it. There was some Latin music playing. I only saw a bartender and two patrons sitting at one of the tables. As soon as we entered, the bartender became animated and hugged Tico. They laughed and exchanged some comments I could barely understand because the music was loud and my ear hadn't tuned in to the local accents and idiomatic expressions of the Ecuadorian people.

I had found my first (and the only) gay bar in Quito. Even though there was no signage outside, the locals referred to it as *El Barcito*. Throughout my stay in Quito, I visited El Barcito several times a week. It had no dance floor or pool table, just a place where gay people could congregate and spend a few precious moments being themselves. I was always amazed how relaxed they seemed knowing that at any moment the *policia* could enter and arrest them all. I wasn't as concerned, as I had a diplomatic passport; the worst that would happen to me would be a scolding.

Tico asked me what I'd like to drink. I'd told him a beer would be fine. He motioned to the bartender to bring me a beer. I noticed immediately that it wasn't cold but at room temperature. Apparently, my expression was obvious. Tico noticed and told me that refrigeration was a luxury and most patrons drank their beer at room temperature. From that point on, whenever I stopped by, they always had several beers tucked away in a small cooler for me. It made me feel very welcome.

Tico explained that even though he was part owner of the bar, it didn't make enough money to support him, so he kept a job at the newspaper to augment his income. The bar, technically illegal in Ecuador at the time, was evidence of entrepreneurial ambitions. We talked a lot that afternoon. I learned he was well educated. His parents, part of the small middle class that existed in Quito, sent him to a university in Texas. After graduation, he returned to Quito and worked at the Banco Central, Ecuador's equivalent to our Federal Reserve Bank. He soon found the work stifling and had a chance to become a beat journalist for the local newspaper, a job much more suited to his outgoing personality.

The UN environment was very open, and there were gay men and women throughout the organization. I became friends with several of them, but I was closest to Tico. We had a short fling, but because our sexual interests were different, we soon agreed that we were better off as friends.

I didn't date or meet many men in my twelve months in Ecuador. Since homosexuality was both illegal and considered highly scandalous, most men were on the down low. It was a bit disheartening. Gay culture seemed as though it was twenty years behind the United States at the time. I wasn't accustomed to the closeted environment and as a result didn't do a lot of dating. As an alternative, I traveled to Miami every two or three months. The flights were rather cheap, and I spent two or three fast and furious days catching up on satisfying my physical needs, returning to Quito satiated and in a much more relaxed frame of mind.

During my entire stay in Ecuador, there was only one guy that I saw on a frequent basis. Tico introduced me to him one night at the bar. His name was Nareem. My friendship with him provided me some of the best memories of my time in Quito. He was West Indian and lived on the Ecuadorian coast with his family. In his early thirties, he was strikingly handsome, with large, almond-shaped eyes and bushy eyebrows. His sensuous lips framed a broad smile, his teeth as white as the sandy beach where he lived. He seemed naturally fit with broad shoulders and a firm round butt and a patch of black chest hair. He had a jet-black complexion that was unblemished except for a heavy beard. His handsome face was framed by a forest of short dreds. The contrast of his darkness against my fair skin was a turn on for both of us.

I was attracted to Nareem not only for his physical charm, but also for his disarming and open personality. His outgoing disposition was more typical of a Caribbean culture than the more passive personalities of the Andean Indian world. We communicated mostly in Spanish since his English was limited. But he was eager to learn and often attempted to comment on something in English, usually resulting in both of us chuckling at his awkward use of words. Nareem's intelligence gave no clue to his impoverished upbringing. He introduced me to a world totally foreign to what I had ever known before. Despite the abject poverty that punctuated the life of he and his family, their spirits remained positive, and they were grateful for the little they did have. They refused to be beaten down by what would most likely be a future with little hope or prosperity. He told me how he struggled to find a job in Quito, support himself, and still send some money and supplies back to his mother, father, and six siblings.

Occasionally, Nareem would take me down to the coast with him on his family visits. During the ten-hour bus trip, we descended from ten thousand feet to sea level. It was like visiting another world.

As we descended from the highlands, the vegetation became lush and tropical, the air thick with humidity. A jungle canopy concealed indigenous creatures calling out with strange sounds. As we got closer to the coast I noticed that people were living in makeshift structures in the trees, high above the ground. From a distance it was a peaceful and picturesque scene, with orchids growing on the limbs of the trees. But I knew that behind the veil of natural beauty, the tree dwellers were trapped in a cycle of terrible poverty with little hope to escape.

Nareem's family was sweet and welcomed me as a special guest. His six brothers and sisters, all younger, hung out around me asking me questions in a mix of Spanish and a coastal Indian language. Nareem would have to translate much of it for me. When Nareem would make subsequent trips back home from Quito, I would often give him a large sack of rice to take with him. As a way to thank me, his mother would send me small handmade baskets that I still had on my bookshelf in Las Vegas.

Although his family generally embraced Christianity, his father was from Brazil and brought with him certain traditions associated with Candomblé. Born of Afro-Brazilian traditions, Candomblé is a polytheistic religion that worships the anima, or soul, of nature—namely, all things that are animal, mineral, and vegetable. Nareem wore a bracelet of jaguar hair on his right wrist, symbolizing various forms of oneness with nature. Looking back, I could see how his spirituality closely resembled that of the native peoples portrayed in the film *Avatar*.

When it came to being intimate, Nareem was uninhibited and very sensual. He loved to have sex on the beach or in the jungle, where he said his spirit felt connected with his natural surroundings. For many of us, there is a boundary between fantasy and reality that we occasionally give ourselves permission to cross. For Nareem, the idea of "fantasy" was a foreign concept, and there were no boundaries. Sex was not a naughty or trashy act. Rather, it was a natural extension of his human behavior, both instinctively animal in its roots and sensual, exotic, and intelligent. His sexual palette was painted by the taste, smell, touch, and sound of his surroundings. His oral exploration during sex was as much an act of discovery as it was to please his partner. While we would each assume dominant and submissive positions, the role play seemed natural and uncontrived. When he would submit to me he would whisper, "que chévere, que chévere"— "how fine, how pleasing." Subsequently, whenever I would hear one of my Hispanic friends use the word "chévere," I'd immediately get a warm rush of memories of my exotic Ecuadorian friend.

After our playful sessions, in a quirky but exotic display, he would kiss his bracelet as a way to acknowledge that we were like the threads of hair on what he called life's bracelet. Nareem introduced me to a sexual freedom that I had never known, a freedom in which the sex act alone was not the prize. I had not experienced that level of physical and spiritual high since that time in Ecuador. Nareem gave me his bracelet during one of the last visits I made to see him. I cherish it to this day as a memory of the special connection we had.

If life's circumstances and timing had been different for both of us, I imagined we could have nurtured a more serious relationship. There were so many layers of Nareem's personality that I wanted to discover. Unfortunately, just before I ended my mission in Quito, his father became ill and he had to quit his job and return home to take care of the family. Even though we kept in touch for a while through Tico, I felt bad that we eventually lost contact. Nareem was exotic and unique, but he was someone I had hoped to meet again someday.

As the months passed, I became a regular at the bar. Each weekend it was expected that I would bring an album of the latest music from the States. I was embarrassed to admit that most of my albums were considered new, even though back home I would have been considered certifiably backward. One rainy evening when the inclement weather deterred even the bravest of souls from coming out for a drink, Tico and I sat alone in the back of the bar listening to one of my old R&B albums. Tico drank his scotch, and I was treated to a refrigerated beer. Despite his intake of scotch, Tico seemed unusually restrained. He kept looking towards the door as if expecting someone to walk in. I finally asked him if he was expecting anyone. He looked at me, his signature smile absent, replaced by locked lips, as if to prevent any air from escaping. I could see in his eyes that he was troubled, if not afraid. I asked him what was bothering him.

Tico explained that a small Ecuadorian gang with connections in Colombia was extorting local businesses for "protection." His partner, an older man who owned banana plantations along the coast, had refused to cooperate with them. Tico explained how Hernan, his partner, often found his car vandalized with slashed tires and smashed windows. This time it was worse. A month earlier he had been found beaten and barely conscious a mile from his country home. He had been stripped of all of his clothing and a symbol was crudely painted on his chest. It was the gang's tag. It was clearly a final warning. Tico said Hernan no longer wanted anything to do with the bar and was basically abandoning his interest. Since then, Tico had agreed to cooperate with the *jefe* of the gang, paying him small amounts every week. He continued, still glancing back occasionally as if expecting the door to open, saying that his weekly payment was small enough right now such that he could continue operating. But he feared in time that their demands would grow. He didn't want to give up the bar. It was his passion, and he felt obligated to his gay brothers to keep it open so they would have somewhere to congregate and enjoy one another's company in private.

The gang was called the Diablos de la Cordillera. "Diablos" translated to "devils," and "cordillera" referred to the spine of the Andes that traversed from north to south down the entire western side of the South American continent. According to Tico, they were a small-town gang but had affiliations with a Colombian counterpart across the nearby border. They didn't deal with the cocaine trade. That was handled by the more sophisticated and well-organized outfits that gave Colombia its reputation as the headquarters for the South American drug cartels. Nevertheless, the Diablos, like many other small local gangs, were capable of instilling fear in small business owners and private citizens.

Tico described their tag as the letters "DC" topped by an outline of the cordillera.

Suddenly, there was a knock on the back door. Tico turned around, almost in a knee-jerk reaction. He got up and asked who was there. "Diablos" was the muffled response. He opened the door. A short, heavyset guy walked in, looking from side to side as if to check out who was there. Tico stiffened up. I assumed it must have been the leader, or *jefe*, of the gang. No words were spoken. Tico led him into the small office in the back. After only a few minutes the jefe came out and exited out the back door. Tico came out shortly afterwards looking somewhat embarrassed that I was there to witness the transaction.

We didn't say much more that evening. We had already had too much to drink. I excused myself and hugged him, reassuring him that I was a good, loyal friend.

We never again had a conversation about what had happened. We remained good friends during my time in Quito, and we eventually thought of one another as brothers. When I returned home to the States, we tried to communicate by e-mail or text at least every month.

❖   ❖   ❖

Having reminisced about my past in Quito, I returned to the present and listened again to Tico's phone message. While it had made me think about my time there nearly ten years ago, I prepared to return his call. I sat down in my comfortable chair as I had a feeling this conversation would be one to warrant being off my feet. His phone didn't ring more than once.

He answered, "Wes, eres tu?"

I said, "Yes, my dear, it's me. What's wrong? Your message sounded as though there was an emergency."

"Wes, they drove me out into the jungle and beat me, then dropped me off at the edge of town by the soccer stadium." Tico said with terror still clinging to his words. "They said next time they won't be so easy on me. An Indian couple bringing potatoes and corn to sell at the market gave me a ride into town after I offered to pay them double what they would make at the market. Wes, it's about the bar. They want more money. I just can't give them any more. What can I do? There's no one in Quito who can help me. They are all afraid of Los Diablos."

Tico coughed and cleared his throat. "They've been intimidating all of the local businesses here for nearly ten years, Wes. It's gotten of hand."

"Calm down, Tico. Let's think this through." I was trying to ease his fears, yet I had no idea what to do.

I asked, "How much time did they give you for the next payment? Can you make one more payment to buy some time until we figure out what to do?"

"Sure, I can make one more payment to cover this month. But after all this time of being under their thumb, I'm out of options. I know they are serious about hurting me, or worse." Tico had an uncharacteristic tremble in his voice.

"Cálmate, chico. We'll figure something out. Did they beat you badly? Are you gonna be okay? "

"I guess. I don't think they broke anything but my spirit. My arms are pretty bruised, but I'll recover." With a nervous laugh he added, "And with my black eyes I look like a raccoon. "

"Well, I'll tell you what. I'm supposed to be in Miami next month. I might be able to get a flight to Quito after my conference. I'm not sure what I can do once I get there, but we have a few weeks to think of something. Sound okay?"

"Oh, Wes, thanks so much. I'm desperate," Tico replied, returning to a more serious tone.

We ended our conversation with our usual good-byes, besos, and abrazos. I couldn't believe I committed to going to Quito at the spur of the moment. I guess the Universe was telling me that my life was going to be anything but routine.

Seven:

⑉ ⑉ ⑉

Dinner's Ready

I needed to go to the gym and settle my nerves down after the conversation with Tico. I took a quick shower first. It was not something I would ordinarily do, but after a night of sex and cuddling with Marcus, respectability demanded a quick rinse. I lotioned up before heading out in to the dry desert air. The gym offered me both physical and emotional toning. I was still in the "rebuilding" phase, having lost some of my muscle mass and tone the past year. But having worked out since I was a teenager, my muscle memory was still responsive to my workouts.

The gym atmosphere in Las Vegas was similar to that in Los Angeles: young people trying to pump up for an evening or afternoon of impressing a prospective partner, and older people trying to hold on to what they had left. It was just a different cast of characters. In LA, there were the wannabe movie and music stars and older folks recovering from the newest facelifts and lipo treatments. In Vegas, a large contingent of the women, young and old, sported the extra and unnatural poundage on their chests so they could compete for the best casino jobs and land the fattest tips. Many of the men sported wild tattoos and haircuts, trying to "out-peacock" their rival bartenders and club managers so as to attract attention and the benefits that often rewarded their efforts.

After my workout, I headed out to the parking lot. I felt a vibration in my bag. Someone was calling. After getting into the car, I reached in the bag and got my phone. The call log listed several numbers, none of which were from the local 702 Las Vegas area code. I recognized most of them, an LA friend checking in and my sis in Chicago. The other number was that of my buddy Angelo. I needed to call him back. It was time for our annual dinner, and I was hosting it in Las Vegas.

❖   ❖   ❖

The phone usually didn't ring more than twice before he would answer. Being the social networker that he was, he couldn't bear missing a call.

"Hey, Bo. How's my bambino doing? I'm looking forward to our dinner next week." Excitement rang in his voice.

"Me too, Nico. Good to hear from you. Are you back in the States?" I asked.

"Yeah, and it's so good to be home. We had a great tour. The band was a big hit in Poland and Austria. I was surprised how much those folks appreciated our funky style."

"Hey, I'm so glad you're back. I haven't seen you in a while," I said, trying to contain my enthusiasm upon hearing his voice again.

"Yeah, and I can't wait to get a good old hamburger and fries … and damn, I don't want to see another cathedral as long as I live. I kept waiting for lightning to strike me down." Angelo bellowed a deep laugh.

Angelo had come to Las Vegas several times to keep me company and help me do some redecorating. He'd loved it out here and said this is the kind of place he wanted when he eventually settled down. He had loved hiking in the desert with me. We'd take a bottle of wine, some Italian bread, and cheese and make a day of it. It was a fertile environment for a musician like him, and he hoped that someday he'd be famous enough to play in one of the big showrooms.

"Wes, I'll be in Vegas the day before the dinner. I have to meet with a guy about replacing our sax player who left the band after the tour ended. I figure I'd come over to the house the night before and help you get set up. Sound okay?"

"That's great, man. I could use the help, and it'll give us time to chill together and catch up. You know it'll be the usual suspects, Clay and—"

Angelo interrupted before I could finish. "I imagine asshole Matthew will be coming, eh? "

"Yes, he'll be here with Clay. They're still together after all these years, somehow, some way."

"Damn, I had hoped someone would have killed the jerk by now." Angelo was not fond of Matthew, not only because of his conservative views but also because Matthew was judgmental about everything.

"No, he's still alive and pissing people off. Say, Daphne called a few days ago and said she could make it too." I said, intentionally getting off the Matthew subject.

"Cool, I was hoping Daph would be able to come out. She's been real busy lately after taking on more clients." Angelo said.

"Angelo, I'm inviting Raul, sort of a new BF from Colombia." Angelo had heard me speak of Raul often, but the two had never met. Uncharacteristic of Angelo, he got quiet for a moment when I mentioned "BF." I figured he was just concerned about me getting with the right guy. He had become a bit protective of me since losing Kevin.

"I look forward to meeting him. You know he'll need my seal of approval." Angelo chuckled.

"That goes without saying, Nico. Say, Emil will be here too. I didn't really expect him to make the drive out here from LA, but I think the dinner gave him an excuse to search the dating sites in Las Vegas."

Angelo laughed, "I'm sure he'll arrange a hookup in Las Vegas. I can only imagine what he'll come across!"

"True, but I think Emil is also looking forward to sparring with Matthew. You know how they detest one another."

Angelo declared, "Hey, I'm onboard that ship."

Though Matthew irritated all of us, we all realized he came with the package, and we all liked Clay too much to exclude them.

I usually counted on Emil to provide some comic relief at the dinner table, although I'd occasionally have to referee the barbs thrown between him and Matthew so things wouldn't get out of hand.

Angelo usually came alone hoping to meet someone and would never forgive me if I didn't invite a single guy to the group. Sometimes he would call the day before and ask me to describe who the "secret guest" might be. It always surprised me that Angelo would look to me to hook him up. With his disarming personality and hot Italian good looks, one would think he would have no problem attracting whomever he wanted. I guess that was the problem. He had too many guys after him. He once told me that he while knew he was attractive, but was insecure about getting close to the guys who were after him. He was always suspicious that they were after one thing and didn't appreciate him for his intelligence. He assumed that most guys thought of musicians as drug-crazed party animals. If they were, he certainly didn't live up to that image. While deep down I know he didn't have expectations of a relationship with most of these blind dates, I think it was more a vicarious way of our connecting with one another. It was odd how we consciously or unconsciously constructed these roles, often for reasons we didn't quite understand. Angelo and I were good examples of that. He respected my past relationships and never tried to come between me and a partner. We seemed to have grown comfortable with the kind of friendship we shared, or at least we acted as though we had.

Angelo inquired, "So Wes, did you find the perfect date for me?"

I had managed to find someone despite the fact I was still relatively new in town.

"Sure did. His name is Will, but no guarantees, okay? Remember what happened last time?" I chuckled at the thought of it.

"Okay, but remember—intelligent, masculine, athletic. I'll take at least two of the three." Angelo laughed but I knew he was serious.

At the last dinner, I invited an old friend who used to compete in the Gay Olympics in track and field. I hadn't spoken with him in a couple of years, but he had sent me an email telling me about the great things that have been happening to him lately. I thought, *Great, I'll invite him to dinner, and maybe he and Angelo would hit it off.* Angelo did run track in college, and they would at least have that in common. Well, the guy came over, and to the shock of all of us, George had become GeorgeAnn. We still had a delightful time, but Angelo would never let me forget.

❖   ❖   ❖

Having completed his business in Las Vegas, Angelo came over that night before the dinner. It had been almost a month since we had seen one another.

"Hey, Baby Bo." Angelo gave me a bear hug and a little slap on the rear. "You're looking more like your old self." He looked as handsome as ever, and his wide grin told me he was glad to be here.

"Hey, I'm so glad you're here. I was afraid you wouldn't be able to get away." I was more excited about Angelo's presence than I let on. This was our first get-together since I moved to Las Vegas, and I was nervous flying solo. I knew that the gathering would be different than the ones before. He provided me the security blanket I needed.

Angelo cocked his head to his side and gave me a half-serious look. "Bo, it was important that I be here, for you and for me."

Feeling an emotional moment about to rush through me, I changed the subject. "So, were you able to take care of your business last night? Is UnderFunk back to 100 percent again?" The members of his band were fun to be around. Back in LA, Angelo occasionally would bring several of them by, and we'd have an impromptu barbecue. They usually appreciated a home-cooked meal after being on the road.

With a big smile on his unshaven face, Angelo replied, "Yep, biz taken care of, and I'm ready to start cookin' wich ya."

We ordered some Chinese for delivery, shared a bottle of wine, and caught one another up on what had been happening the past month. But we were both tired and made an early evening of it. As Angelo was headed to his room, he grabbed me by the arm and turned me around to face him.

His face had little expression. With his lips closed but relaxed he transmitted a calmness that filled me with warmth. With his eyes slightly squinting he asked, "Bo, are you really doing okay?"

With my eyes starting to well with tears I looked away and just hugged him. I mumbled, "Nico, it's been so hard. Sometimes I feel so empty and lost."

Angelo gently cupped my face in his large hands and whispered. "Wes, you'll get through this, and I'll be there for you every step of the way." He pulled my face into his chest and rubbed my neck. I could smell him and feel the warmth of his body close to me. I felt safe.

Even though Angelo had his own room to stay in, he insisted on lying next to me that night. I sensed he needed it as much as I did.

❖   ❖   ❖

We got up early the next morning. In several hours, the heat of the day would arrive with scorching intensity. Angelo sat down on one of the patio lounges. I brought out coffee for both of us and joined him on the lounge.

"Wes, it's so good to be here with you. It feels like home here, you know?" He was stretched across the lounge with his arms behind his head. Wearing only his boxers and a tank top, he seemed to offer his hairy legs and armpits as emblems of his masculinity.

I was about to respond when two hummingbirds hovered near us at one of the feeders I had hung. Angelo turned his head slightly and I could see an easy smile grow on his face as he watched the pair sample the nectar.

"Cute, aren't they?" I said, slightly embarrassed that he noticed I had been staring at him and not the hummingbirds.

Sitting up and trying to be subtle about rearranging his "stuff" contained in his boxers, he said, "Yeah, cute, happy, and natural."

I picked up my mug and finished the last drop of coffee. "Want a fill-up, Nico? I asked.

"No, Wes. I'm fine." He stared out into the garden, motionless, as though a peace had descended upon him.

As I got up to get more coffee he asked, "Where you goin'?"

"Just to get a refill," I said.

"Hurry back," he said thoughtfully.

I went into the kitchen smiling.

We sat for another half hour not saying anything, but it was obvious we were enjoying one another's company.

Angelo tugged on my arm. "Hey, Bo, we best get busy and get

things set up for the dinner. If I sit here any longer, I may just turn into a useless loaf."

Trying to stop my mind from drifting to where it shouldn't, I responded, "No chance of that, my friend. Let's get to work."

It was going to be a warm evening, so we moved the dining table outside on the patio. I was very proud of the garden. The desert plants and lighting made for a wonderful atmosphere, and many of the cacti were in full bloom, sporting flowers of bright reds, purples, oranges, and yellows. Angelo loved decorating, so I left the table-setting up to him. He collected some flowers and branches from the garden and made a beautiful centerpiece. He even made individual flower vases using some of my shot glasses and floated a white flower from some blooming yucca plants in each one. It always tickled me that this masculine man had such a sensitive side to him which he revealed to few people.

❖   ❖   ❖

Our traditional quarterly dinners were simple affairs, more intended to bring us together than to satisfy some grand culinary urge. This would be the first time the group of usual suspects would meet outside of the friendly confines of Hollywood—and the first time I would be attending as a single man. I looked forward to the companionship and the chance to be with my old friends without having to go back to LA and deal with all the memories that were still too fresh to make a visit enjoyable. Our dinner was especially important to me this time, representing a thread of continuity in a fabric otherwise tugged, stretched, stressed, and occasionally ripped by life's wear. We were a diverse if not a slightly dysfunctional group to be breaking bread together. But we were all connected, sometimes for less than flattering reasons, by the so-called six degrees of separation. In some of our cases, it was considerably less than six degrees.

It was nearly eight years ago, we started out as three couples: Kevin and I, Matthew and Clay, and Angelo and whoever his date happened to be. The young and flamboyant Emil became a regular after we first invited him several years ago. He was single and provided the comic relief that we often needed. The group was rounded out by Daphne. Over time, the dinner list went through various changes. Occasionally, a new guest would be invited but usually they were never invited back, more often than not because they weren't genuinely interested in connecting with us as a "family." Angelo no longer brought a date with him. He had pretty much dropped out of the dating scene since all his energy went into his band.

The only real constant was Matthew and Clay, the most unlikely couple to have withstood the eight years of our tradition—and one another. Yet their years of "wedded bliss" were cratered with separations and reconcilements. The breakups and makeups usually coincided with political elections or some major social events that created the appropriate stew for their basic philosophical, political, and social differences to come to a boil. Matthew was ultraconservative, born of German parents from upstate New York. Clay was a proud black man from Philadelphia who devoted his life to political advocacy for the LGBT community and black gay men, in particular. They seemed oddly comfortable playing adversarial roles in their relationship. Angelo, Daphne, and I, who were nearly ten years their senior, figured we were older and wiser, and each year claimed it would never last. Yet Clay and Matthew repeatedly proved us wrong.

Matthew was a gorgeous, masculine man. He had an athletic body, not overly built but with a low body fat count that most would envy. He was an amateur boxer in his late teens and still maintained his lean tone. On the downside, he was ultraconservative and was not shy about volunteering his opinions. During our political arguments we'd occasionally credit his radical views to the numerous concussions he must have suffered in the ring. I had always figured his choice of partners, the ultra-liberal and social activist, Clay, reflected an internal conflict between what he wanted to be vs. what he was. Clay was the intellect and looked every bit like a professor. Clay worked with many groups as a consultant and authored several books about the impact of HIV in the gay minority community. I always thought Clay was handsome, and I think the attraction was mutual, but 'hooking up' was never meant to be.

Many years before he met Clay, I was introduced to Matthew when he was in LA on vacation, before his move from Miami. At the time, he was a manager at Turkey Point Nuclear Power Plant in South Florida, later being transferred to San Onofre, just south of LA. We played around once. Yes, he was handsome and hot, but the sex was strange, mechanical, and a bit selfish—or at least that's what I recalled after all those years. Angelo had confessed years ago that he had been with Matthew once as well and shared the same opinion of him. Matthew and I remained friends, but I always felt we never got really close because of our diametrically opposed political and social views. Even though he was flawed, he had a heart of gold if you were his friend, and he would stop at nothing to help you.

It was at a party over ten years ago where I introduced Matthew to Clay. Even as I warned Clay of this conservative time bomb, Clay insisted on meeting him. I guess the hormones won the battle over intellect that night. None of us ever really understood the relationship between Clay and Matthew, but love worked in strange ways. Besides, we figured the make-up sex after they argued must be hot. The universe brought them together through me, and I never questioned Mother Universe! They'd been together ever since.

Emil was one of my more unconventional friends who Kevin and I met in a most unconventional way. It was about five years ago, and Emil was only 19 years old. Kevin and I had just finished eating at a restaurant in West Hollywood. While I waited to settle the bill,

Kevin walked down the street to have a smoke. When I came out I heard this scuffling and yelling, and towards the end of the block I saw Kevin in a fight with several guys. Even though Kevin was strong for his size he was overwhelmed by two big thugs who had him pinned to the sidewalk. Suddenly, out of nowhere, Emil ran up and tore through the two attackers like they were school children. By the time I got there Emil had beaten the guys off, leaving one limping as he tried to run away. "Go home to your mommies!" he yelled, snapping his fingers at them as they ran off into the night. We became fast friends.

Emil was tall and muscular, yet he was as flamboyant a gay man as you could know. His outlandish clothes and effeminate speech and gestures disguised the tough man underneath. He was fair skinned but his features reflected the heritage of his white mother and black father. Originally from New York City, he maintained a close relationship with his father, a retired boxer. Given the homophobic nature of professional sports, Emil moved to the West Coast as a teenager with his mother to escape the spotlight surrounding his father so he could live his life more openly. He got a job writing a social column for one of the gay magazines in LA. A year ago on a visit back to New York, his father, long divorced, confessed that he himself had been on the down low for years, and upon his recent retirement had decided to write a tell-all book. While I had never met him, Emil had shown me pictures of his father during the peak of his boxing career. That man could have set fire to his own clothes just by standing still!

I loved Emil dearly, and through his flamboyant and comical antics he was often the voice of reality and reason. There were times when the boys at dinner would get in to deep philosophical arguments, each believing he was more profound than the other. Then suddenly, Emil would interrupt with some off-the-wall comment that would make everyone laugh but also would contain some element of truth. The effect was to deflate all egos at the table and redirect the conversation to a totally new topic. The conservative Matthew had only disdain for Emil, finding it hard to imagine why a man would display such effeminate traits. I always presumed this attitude was born out of his own insecurities as a gay man.

I didn't know Angelo's blind date, Will, very well. He was a personal trainer at the gym where I worked out. He seemed friendly and outgoing, and had a sculpted body that was evidence of hours at the gym each day. I hoped that he and Angelo might find a connection. Will frequently talked about how involved he was in the local community. I had assumed he meant causes such as HIV/AIDS advocacy or assistance to the homeless. Although I didn't know it at the time, it turned out it couldn't have been further from the truth.

❖   ❖   ❖

I eagerly anticipated the dinner, but now that the time had arrived, I was a bit nervous. I wanted things to continue as they had always been, but I knew that wouldn't be entirely possible. I prepared myself for a different experience, telling myself that it would be different and that this wasn't necessarily a bad thing. Having Angelo cohost made all the difference. As my best friend he provided the continuity in my life that I wanted and needed. He was always there to reassure me, to tell me when I was off track, and to celebrate successes and find lessons in failures.

Angelo came out of his room looking like a model out of *GQ*.

I teased him. "Hey, Rico Suave, you're going to catch something on fire looking like that."

Wearing a V-neck T-shirt and washed-out jeans slung low on his narrow hips, Angelo played up the part. "Yeah, man, I'm out to conquer and divide today, and maybe I should start with the host."

Feigning a protest I replied, "That's all well and good, but first get your sassy butt in the kitchen and bake those rolls you've been bragging about."

Angelo started to posture like a thug and was about to grab me when the doorbell rang.

It was Raul. He was wearing jeans, a polo shirt, and his signature baseball cap. We hugged and gave each other a warm kiss. At first I was reluctant to invite Raul into this inner circle. After all, I hadn't known him that long. None of the other guys had met him yet, although I had described him to Angelo. I was hoping he'd fit in with the "family."

I put my arm around Raul's stocky frame. "Hey, babe, good to see you."

Raul tilted his head down in a shy pose I hadn't seen before. "Beto, how are you doing? I'm glad I could make it, although I'm a little nervous about meeting your friends."

Just then, Angelo came over. Always one to make a person comfortable, Angelo gave him a warm greeting and hug. "Nice to meet you, man. Wes has told me a lot about you. From what I know, he's a lucky man."

Raul blushed and replied, "I think I'm the lucky one." That pleased Angelo, as he always felt he needed to protect me from ill-intended wannabe boyfriends. Angelo gave me a quick wink, as if signaling his approval.

Raul took his small overnight bag to our bedroom. Since he had spent a lot of time at the house and had left some clothes and toiletries there, there wasn't much to bring.

No sooner had Raul come back out of the bedroom than Clay and Matthew arrived. I knew they would be on time. Even though Clay was the disorganized one of the two, Matthew was his polar opposite, providing Clay the structure he needed. Conversely, Clay provided a safe channel for Matthew to occasionally "get wild."

Given our mutual experiences in sleeping with Matthew years ago, Angelo and I would laugh as we imagined what "getting wild" would mean for Matthew.

Not surprisingly, they were both arguing about something as they came through the door.

"Hey guys, you—" My greeting was interrupted by two bear hugs from both of them. "You guys always look the same. Thanks for coming to Sin City. Time to put a little spice in our men's dinner, eh?" I was trying to make a joke, but only Clay smiled.

Clay was dark-skinned and had a head of thick, black hair trimmed very short. He was slight in frame but still looked fit. Nearly a foot shorter than Angelo, Clay's head barely reached Angelo's chest when he leaned over to give him a hug.

"How you been, Holmes?" Angelo playfully said to Clay.

"All's good, man. I'm hearing so many good things about you and that wicked guitar," Clay answered.

"Yeah, you know, I'm so lucky. I've been having a ball doing what I love," Angelo said proudly.

In his deep voice, Matthew formally acknowledged Angelo and reluctantly shook his hand. "Hello, Angelo."

Matthew looked drop-dead handsome as usual. He had deep blue eyes that could lure you in like a bated hook. His wavy, light brown hair was cut short.

The two had never been close except for the time they slept together years ago. Matthew always seemed to think less of Angelo because of his choice of careers, and Angelo was offended by Matthew's conservative arrogance. Both would give anything to be able to erase the little tryst from their past.

Angelo just nodded and said nothing to Matthew.

I introduced Raul to Clay. Displaying his signature compassion for others and gracious manner, Clay said, "It's nice to meet you, Raul. From what Wes has told me about you, it sounds like you have an interesting background. I've always wanted to visit your country."

"Thanks, Clay. I'm fortunate, I guess, that I've had some great career opportunities. I wouldn't have met Ewwwes otherwise." Raul struggled with the "W" in my name.

Clay was never self-centered in his interactions with others. Instead, he always demonstrated interest in what people were doing and thinking. I could tell his greeting put Raul at ease.

That wasn't the case with Matthew. Although polite with a handshake, he greeted Raul with a sense of aloofness, just nodding and not really making eye contact. Matthew often was reserved and quiet around strangers, especially those of different cultural backgrounds. Raul picked up on his cool reception but turned his attention to Angelo who returned to the kitchen.

"Hey, Angelo, how about some help with those avocados?" Raul followed Angelo into the kitchen."

"Wes, there's no way we would let these get-togethers disappear. It's great to be here," Clay said. "The house looks beautiful. The yard is, as I imagined, gorgeous, and not a single weed!"

I smiled. Clay knew how obsessed I was about the garden, but he also acknowledged how therapeutic it was for me, especially now.

"You guys doing well?" I asked. My expression must have conveyed some doubt.

Clay looked over his glasses and responded, "Well, yeah, you know, little train wrecks here and there, but Matthew and I usually get back on track. I've been doing a lot of traveling to D.C. lately for black HIV/AIDS advocacy meetings. You know, you think we make progress in getting legislative and committee support for more funding, but then the far right pulls the other direction. I'm still hopeful we'll prevail."

Avoiding any further discussion about their marital challenges, I commented, "You know I'm so proud of you, Clay. I wish I had your courage."

"Thanks, Wes. You know I'm always on a mission, but hey, enough of the serious stuff. How about one of those margaritas you've been bragging about?"

At that moment, Angelo came through the kitchen door with a handful of cut flowers from the garden. He was grinning as if he had just discovered gold in the back yard.

With a toothy smile big enough to disarm even the most formidable opponent, Clay joked, "Looks like you haven't lost your decorating touch. That *Martha Stewart Living* subscription must be paying off!"

Angelo laughed and said, "Yeah, imagine if you would have sent me *Hunters: Guns and Ammo*?"

I took Clay and Matthew for a quick tour of the house and led them out to the patio.

"It's beautiful here, Wes," Matthew said as he pointed to all the cacti blooming by the pool. "I can see why you call it your sanctuary."

I said, "Yep, it's my little piece of heaven and an escape from civilization."

Matthew said, "Clay and I need a place like this. It would give us peace."

Without thinking, I said, "Matthew, you have to make your own peace. It doesn't just happen."

Matthew shook his head as if to say, *"yeah, right."* Clay tried to ignore my comment.

I knew they argued a lot, but I sensed that Matthew was on edge.

I left a pitcher of margaritas and some chips and salsa on the patio table.

"Make yourself comfortable, guys. I need to do a few things inside." I figured they were probably a bit hungry from the four-hour drive from LA.

I went back inside to warm up the paella that I had made early in the morning. Raul was making a sangria recipe he knew from Colombia, and Angelo was busy chopping tomatoes and cucumbers for the salad. They were both joking and laughing.

"Glad to see that the two chefs are getting along in the kitchen!" I shouted.

They put their arms around one another, and Raul answered, "Yes, I'm training my assistant."

Angelo pretended to protest and said, "Hell no, I've taught him everything he knows in the past fifteen minutes."

I just laughed at both of them and said, "Seems to me you both have been sampling the sangria."

Then, like a little kid tugging at my sleeve, Angelo leaned over to me. "Bo, when is Mr. Right going to arrive?" he asked, obviously referring to the blind date I was obligated to invite.

"Don't worry yourself, sweet thing. The package will arrive soon," I said reassuringly. Just then there was a knock on the door.

Angelo and I both walked to the front door. It was Daphne.

I reached out and grabbed her hands and greeted her, "Girl, Angelo and I were hoping you could make it! You look great."

She did look terrific. Daphne had two looks. One was the hair-in-a-bun, lawyered-up look. The other, which she wore that day, had her long red hair flowing freely over a silky green blouse. Around her neck she wore a beaded neck band that gave her a bit of a bohemian look. She gave each of us a hug and kiss.

"Hey, sweetie, no one riding shotgun with you today?" Angelo always kidded her about never bringing a friend with her. While she dated occasionally, she still had fears about committing that she's never been able to overcome.

"Nope, still sassy and single. As long as I got you two guys I figure I'm ahead of the game." She winked and added, "I have been seeing a guy who lives in Julian, in the mountains just east of San

Diego. He has a small ranch and trains horses, but hasn't been able to train me yet, and you know I don't like anyone telling me what to do." We all laughed.

"Well, that should prove to be an interesting partnership," I said with a touch of sarcasm. "We already have one dysfunctional couple here. We may have to build an octagon on the patio and put all you guys in it to settle your differences." Angelo imitated a boxer. We all bent over with laughter.

"Actually, he's very sweet and open-minded. You'd like him a lot. I met him through the office. He came in to get some legal advice regarding new zoning in Julian that could impact his ranch. I invited him, but he didn't have anyone available to watch over the ranch."

"Cool. Get comfortable, lawyer girl. I'll put your bag in the other guest room." I took her bag to the other spare bedroom. The house would be full for the first time. It had three bedrooms and a den with a sofa bed—just enough room to accommodate everyone.

Angelo and Daphne sat in the living room to catch up on what'd been going on since they last saw one another. They happily sipped the margaritas that were waiting for them.

There was another knock on the door. I tried to hide the surprise evident on my face as Emil and Will, Angelo's blind date, walked in together. Apparently, everyone shared the same feeling of wonderment as this unlikely duo made their entrance.

Both Will and Emil were tall and well built, but Will appeared every bit the masculine hunk and Emil was wearing white jeans, an orange tank top, lime tennis shoes, and a bandanna.

Seeing the surprised looks on our collective faces, Will stepped aside as if to distance himself from Emil and proclaimed defensively, "Oh no, we just met out front and realized we're both going to the same place."

"Ah, c'mon, Mr. Will, tell the truth. We've been seeing each other secretly for months now." Emil joked with a smug look. He gave Will a faux hug and patted him on the butt as they came through the door.

We all laughed, hoping Will would see through Emil's playfulness.

"Hi, Em. I'm glad you could make it out to the provinces." I gave him a solid hug.

"Ooh, Papa Bear, you keep huggin' me like that and we'll have to cancel dinner and go straight, I mean directly, to dessert!" Emil liked to clown but he was grateful for our friendship as was I.

Emil quickly looked around, wanting to avoid Matthew for as long as possible. They were like the crazy uncle and misguided nephew. They didn't get along but were like family nevertheless, and neither was denied their place at the table.

I introduced Will to Angelo.

"Nice to meet you, Angelo," Will said in a reserved tone, all the while checking Angelo out from top to bottom. Will's tight jeans and Under Armour shirt highlighted every twitching muscle in his torso. He was a tall, cool glass of water.

"Same here, Will. I hear you're a personal trainer. Looks like your practice what you preach." Angelo sported a provocative smile and let one hand hang off the belt of his jeans.

"I try." Will stood erect, as though trying to make himself taller than he actually was.

Angelo introduced Daphne. "This is Daphne, a close friend from our days in Chicago."

Will acknowledged Daphne with a sort of cocky arrogance, pursing his lips and raising his eyebrows, as if to say, "nice looking chick." Daphne, a bit put off, just replied with a hello and returned to the living room. Fortunately, Angelo had turned around and missed the odd exchange.

Raul brought out a big pitcher of margaritas. I introduced him to Will, Emil, and Daphne. Will greeted Raul with a quick hello.

Daphne was more engaging. "Raul, Wes has told me a lot about you. You know, I spent six months as a high school exchange student in Bogota."

I looked at Daphne and remarked, "Hey, we've got a little South American connection going on here."

Raul had a relaxed smile on his face, clearly pleased and relaxed at having met Daphne.

Emil gave Raul a hug and, with his hands on his hips, said, "Don Raul, do you have a twin brother down there in Colombia? If so, I could sure roast some coffee beans with him!"

Raul just laughed, having been forewarned about Emil's crazy but endearing outbursts.

"I have five brothers, and a twin who is gay," Raul said with a suggestive smile.

Emil put his hand on his forehead as if ready to faint and walked away. "Bring the ice!"

Everyone laughed. Once Emil got that six-foot-two frame in motion, there was no telling what would happen.

Emil grabbed Raul by the hand and said, "Wesley, show us around the estate."

Raul smiled and went along for the ride.

We walked around past the pool. There was a faux desert wash with rocks and cacti that emptied out onto a small lawn surrounded by mesquite trees.

Emil waved his arm from left to right as if blessing the yard. "Wes, honey, I'm gonna have my wedding here. All my exes can stand over there with those nasty cactus and the ceremony will be down in that cute grassy area."

Raul laughed when Emil pointed to him and lip synched, *"This one"*.

We walked back to the house, except for Emil who joked and said he wanted to spend a little more time planning his outdoor wedding.

Angelo and Will were sitting on the couch making small talk.

I interrupted, "Why don't you and Will grab a margarita and get comfortable? Raul and I can get the food ready."

I watched them both walk out to the back patio, hoping that they would hit it off. Angelo turned around and gave me a little wink. I shot him back a quick thumbs-up.

Raul helped me get the food ready to serve. The aroma of the saffron in the paella filled the house as I carried it through the kitchen and family room out to the dining table on the patio. Raul went back to the kitchen and brought out the salad and the fresh rolls. I paused for a moment and took a deep breath.

Raul asked, "Are you doing okay, Beto?" He rubbed my back with his hand.

I said, "Yeah, Raul, thanks. I'm good."

Raul understood what the dinner meant to me and how this time it was going to be different from all the others. He did his best to make sure I felt the security and warmth of his companionship, and I did.

We called everyone to dinner.

❖　　❖　　❖

I had a long, narrow dining table made of recycled barn wood. It was rustic and country-looking but very accommodating for a large group. I sat at one end with Raul next to me. Next to Raul were Clay and Matthew. Will and Angelo sat across from them. Emil and Daphne sat at the other end.

We always started dinner with the same toast. I said, "Let's be grateful for being able to enjoy this dinner with good friends and also remember those who are no longer with us." The toast was more impactful this time, for obvious reasons. Clay and Matthew threw quick glances my way but I focused on the table in front of me. Raul, understanding the significance, gently squeezed my leg under the table.

Clay initiated conversation by commenting, "Wes, you seem to be adjusting well to life out here in the provinces. Seriously, you look good. I know it's been hard."

I appreciated Clay's thoughtfulness and responded, "Thanks, Clay. I'm doing well. I figure it'll take a full year to really see if I'm going to stay here. I'll know my options better then."

Clay inquired, "So what's this about you going back to Quito for business?"

I had mentioned to Clay weeks earlier that I was going back but didn't give any details.

I explained, "My friend, Tico, who runs a small gay bar, is having problems with some thugs who are extorting him for protection. He got beat up pretty bad and wanted me to help him settle affairs."

Matthew injected himself into the conversation, "Damn, you sure you want to get involved in some mess in a foreign country?" He had a way of making his questions sound like interrogations.

Feeling put on the defensive, I responded, "Tico was my best friend when I worked down there. He helped me get settled and adjusted. I figure I'll be in Miami for meetings next month, and it's not a long flight from there." I looked at Matthew and knew what was coming.

Angelo gave me a quick glance and motioned with his hands as though he was buckling his seat belt.

"I wouldn't go near the place. You know South America is known for all its gang activity and drug cartels. Crazy lunatics run those countries." Matthew put on a condescending expression that I had seen many times before.

Emil chimed in, "Matthew, my dear, let me remind you about the gang-infested streets of LA—and whose car was found in a gang chop shop?" he asked, referencing Matthew's BMW that was stolen a year ago.

Matthew tried to ignore Emil's comment and escalated the conversation to include Raul. "Raul, is the Colombian government still losing the battle with the drug cartels?"

Raul, clearly bothered by the question but not wanting to engage Matthew, responded, "It's been a challenge, but things have changed greatly in Colombia. The government is in firm control, and there is little violence that affects the general public." The pink in Raul's cheeks gave away his increasing discomfort with the direction in which the discussion was headed.

Matthew was about to respond, but Clay subtly grabbed Matthew's wine glass and handed it to him. This had become an almost subconscious maneuver by Clay to signal to Matthew that it was time to shut up. As awkward as it sounded, it was usually effective. Earlier, when setting the table, Angelo had joked about making sure that Matthew's wine glass was positioned within easy reach of Clay.

Angelo and Will were rather quiet. I wasn't sure yet if they were making a connection. Angelo had season tickets to the Gay Men's Chorus and invited Will to their performance the following weekend. He said he could stay the weekend with him in LA. Unfortunately, Will seemed unimpressed by the invitation. In fact, he didn't seem very engaging throughout much of the dinner. Nevertheless, Angelo tried to maintain a pleasant dialogue with Will. Amidst the subsequent debates between Matthew and everyone else, it was hard to tell if Will was really being receptive. Time would tell. I noticed Will seemed to stare at Daphne occasionally. While Daphne was polite, she didn't acknowledge his glances. Angelo still didn't seem to pick up on his behavior.

Raul went back to the kitchen to refill the pitchers of sangria.

Clay, leaning forward, whispered to me and said, "Wes, so what's the story with this young twenty-two-year-old you've adopted?"

I put my fingers over my lips, instructing everyone to hush.

After all, I was dating Raul. "The papers haven't gone through yet," I joked, quietly. "Hey, he was just what I needed, and I seemed to have filled a need for him too." Everyone laughed at the double entendre.

"Good for you," Clay said approvingly. "Young blood is probably what the doctor ordered for you right now."

"Well, I've cooled it a bit with him since I met Raul."

Raul came back to the table, fortunately missing the last few minutes of the conversation.

Emil announced that he was going to Brazil the following month. He was quite proud that an older guy from LA was taking him on an exotic vacation.

"When I hit the Copacabana in my bikini even the macho guys will want a piece of auntie Em." Emil had a proud grin on his face.

Matthew, shaking his head, responded, "Yeah, letting a sugar daddy take care of you is like prostitution."

Emil countered with conviction, "Hey, as long as papa gets what he wants I seal the deal, baby."

For the first time, Will surprisingly engaged in the discussion. "There isn't anything wrong with paying for sexual services. If it benefits everyone involved, then no harm, no foul."

Angelo and I gave one another a quick look as if to say, "*What, now he joins the table discussion?!*"

Matthew, eager to lob another salvo at Emil exclaimed, "Emil, if you're going to attract those hot Brazilian studs, you'll need to butch it up a bit."

I thought, "*Oh, no, here it comes.*"

While Emil's reddish brown dreds made his head look like it was on fire, the real heat came from the verbal flames that he could spew on cue.

"Well, sweet thing, at least I can man up and talk like a jock if I want. I'm not sure what can be done to improve that nasty-ass personality of yours." Emil mimicked a hyper-masculine demeanor. "Just 'cause you got "chestacles" doesn't make you a man."

At that moment, the cuckoo clock on my wall sounded the hour. It was the comic relief we all needed, as the discussion was getting a bit out of control. By the time the crazy bird said its last cuckoo, everyone had erupted in laughter.

But Matthew had to have the last word and called Emil a "mistake of nature." Even before Clay could reach for Matthew's wine glass, Emil countered, "No, baby, I'm a miracle. With all my problems, I'm still probably one of the happiest guys at this table." The truth in that statement wasn't lost on anyone that evening.

"Okay, boys, back to your corners," I announced, waiving my hands like a referee at a fight.

In an effort to redirect the discussion, I asked Clay what events were on his calendar for the remainder of the year. He talked about the several conferences he planned to attend. He mentioned a training initiative he was asked to lead for several large police organizations on the East Coast. The sessions addressed diversity, with an emphasis on minority populations served by primarily white police forces. Being Trinidadian, gay, and HIV-positive, Clay could provide a perspective that could be helpful to those organizations serving diverse constituencies.

Daphne had at one time provided free legal services to several LGBT organizations in San Diego. Trying to raise the level of conversation above all the trash talk that seemed to dominate the table, she said, "Clay, it's possible that my firm might be able to help sponsor your awards banquet this coming winter. You'll have to send me whatever you have so I can have our public relations liaison follow up."

Clay, clearly pleased, exclaimed, "Wow, that's great, Daphne! You know, this year we have some big celebrities participating. It would be good exposure for you guys, and of course, we always need the support."

Angelo chimed in, "Clay, we're so proud of you. I imagine what you'll have to say will rattle some cages, but that's a good thing."

Given the topic of conversation, I was expecting Will to chime in since he had indicated to me how involved he was with the community. But again, he seemed oddly disconnected from our conversation.

Matthew added, "I know Clay's a great trainer, and his perspective is certainly a healthy one. But I think there should be training as well for some of these minority groups, especially those who don't bother to learn English. They need to know what the expectations are in order to become integrated into our society."

Raul squirmed in his chair, wanting to say something, but then decided to be polite. I told him later that I would have respected anything he would have said and in the future not to hold back.

Angelo didn't hold back, however. "Matthew, implying that people with different backgrounds don't deserve the same things in life is wrong. Believing that these cultural differences are damaging is ignorant. Diversity makes us stronger." Angelo's face was getting red.

At this point, Daphne was gripping the end of the table and couldn't hold back. "You know, Matthew, I spent two years in the Peace Corps in Africa. I agree that other cultures sometimes have customs that seem silly or even offensive to us."

A smile was starting to form on Angelo's blushing face as Daphne continued.

"But you know, for many nonnatives, our customs not only seem odd, but our Western culture often appears to be intolerant, competitive, and unforgiving." Daphne spoke with a commanding presence that had everyone listening. But her calm and deliberate demeanor helped to remove the vitriol from the conversation.

Raul tapped me on the leg under the table measuring his approval. I smiled back.

Showing an unusual moment of restraint, Matthew didn't

respond. I think he realized he may have gone a bit too far. But, of course, he would never step up to apologize. Clay and I both sighed with relief that the conversation didn't escalate. Matthew was getting on everyone's nerves. He was always confrontational, but this evening he was unusually sour, leading some of us to think that there may be problems between him and Clay.

I motioned for Clay to come back and help me with something in the kitchen.

I asked Clay, "Hey, why does Matthew seem so bitter tonight? He's really getting on everyone's last nerve."

For the first time in a long while, Clay looked beaten down. "I'm sorry, Wes. These past few months for us have been very difficult. You know Matthew's been estranged from his family for a long time. They're conservative Christians and missionaries for their church and haven't been able to accept his lifestyle. After all these years, Matthew tried to reconcile with them, but they told him they don't want anything to do with him and not to contact them again. He was deeply hurt and angry. I encouraged him to get professional help. I hope he does, because he's becoming difficult to be around."

I just shook my head. "I feel bad for both of you, Clay. Is there anything I can do? Are you okay?"

"Yeah, bud, hopefully Matthew will work through it. I'm traveling more now so that's good in some ways, sort of a balance between being there for him and giving me some space."

Afterward, I felt a bit more empathy for Matthew. I couldn't dismiss his irascible behavior, but I thought maybe I could find ways to engage him on a more positive basis in the future.

Clay and I returned to the table. Matthew shot us both a quick glare as if he knew we had a conversation about him. I didn't acknowledge it and continued eating.

For a short while the conversation was less contentious. Matthew mellowed out after Clay refilled his wine glass several times. Emil seemed occupied, checking his phone for e-mail messages from one of his sex sites.

Daphne, who could hold her own in any debate, wouldn't hesitate handing you your ass on a platter if that was what was required to make her point. Tonight, however, she held back, even though I knew she was tempted several times to enter the fray.

At one point toward the end of dinner, I overheard Emil and Daphne talking about fashion. I heard Emil comment, "Well, girl, you sure have it goin' on, but unfortunately havin' sex with a woman doesn't seem fun to me at all."

We all glanced at the cuckoo clock hoping it would sound its acknowledgement of Emil's crazy comment.

Daphne, who during the evening had grown fond of Emil's quirky and uninhibited ways, quickly responded with a little smile, "Well, my dear, that's why you're gay." Everyone chuckled, even Emil.

Will, who remained quiet throughout most of the evening except for his odd comment on the sex industry, seemed unaffected by all the debate and argument until Matthew hit on a subject close to home.

At one point during the lull in conversation, Matthew directed a flirtatious glance towards Will.

In a judgmental tone, Matthew said, "Clay and I are going to move to a different gym. We're getting tired of the queens wearing their matching outfits and trying to pump up for dates that will probably never have a happy conclusion."

I heard Emil grunt a disapproving, "Hmmm", assuming Matthew had made reference to him.

Raul, in an attempt to engage a bit more asked, "Emil, how do you keep such a nice body?"

Emil swooned at the compliment and replied. "I used to be a gymnast in college."

Daphne inquired, "Do you still do gymnastics?"

Emil paused, and shook his head, "Well, dear, not the kind you're referring to but I still stick my landings!"

Everyone roared except Matthew who flashed a look of disapproval.

Matthew, who had a fabulous body under those baggy clothes, continued, "Gay gyms are nothing more than meat markets. Personally, I work out just to relieve stress."

Will, who fit every bit the image of a narcissistic gym rat with his skin tanned to the correct shade of hotness so as to accentuate the veins in his biceps, agreed with Matthew.

He claimed, "I go mainly to relieve emotional stress as well. It allows me to be a more positive member of the community and make a contribution to my clients' wellness."

It struck me as odd that for the first time that evening, someone actually was agreeing with Matthew. Angelo had a strained look on his face but took the high road and remained silent.

It was at this moment that Emil, waving his finger in the air, interrupted, saying, "Oh, my, the caca is getting deep in here."

Directing a probing comment at Will he continued, "And, my dear, I thought you looked familiar. I noticed you have a personal ad in 'Out & About in Las Vegas' magazine … in the naughty section, if I remember correctly."

Will lifted up his wine glass and took a long sip, as if contemplating a response.

Emil continued, "And that photo, my goodness. Hallelujah for stress reduction!" Everyone froze during what was one of the more awkward moments of the evening. Both Matthew and Will remained silent. Stunned was more like it.

Angelo was quietly relishing the moment and pinched me under the table.

I could see Clay put his hand on Matthew's leg as if to say, *"Cool it, honey"*, but it was too late.

Matthew muttered under his breath just loud enough so that Emil could hear. "Like father like son."

I thought Emil's dreds were going to stand straight up as he tensed up and gripped the edge of the table with both hands.

"Yeah, Papa's stone has rolled over to the other side of the room. So what? What IS your problem, man?" Emil, with fire in his eyes, looked directly across at Matthew.

Matthew replied in an arrogant tone, "All women in the family, I guess."

Emil jumped out of his chair, knocking over his wine, and posturing as if to pounce on Matthew.

There was dead silence. The only thing moving was the water in the glasses, sloshing from the impact when Emil sprung out of his chair. Angelo rushed up behind Emil, prepared to restrain him, but Emil gestured for him to sit down.

"I'm ok gentlemen." Losing all his feminine affectation, the veins in his face swelling, and shaking a fist instead of his usual parade wave, Emil continued. "This bloviating blowhole needs to check himself. I don't have to apologize for me or my father."

For a moment, in his rage, I thought Emil looked much like his father during his fighting days.

Emil threw his napkin on his chair and directed his final comment directly at Matthew. "I'll tell you one thing my radioactive friend", referring to his work at the nuclear plant, "I'm more man than you'll ever be, and more woman than you could ever have."

With that, Emil left the table and headed out to the garden.

After a moment, Matthew got up and went to his room. The defeated look on his face made me think he was somewhat impressed by the real man that emerged from underneath Emil's flaming persona.

Clay looked at me and shook his head in disgust. I winked at him as if to say, *"It's okay."* He soon got up to check on Matthew.

No one spoke for several minutes.

Breaking the icy silence I quipped sarcastically, "Well, that went well."

Angelo responded, "I don't know what "bloviating" means but it doesn't sound good."

I added, "Trust me, it's not."

Everyone chuckled nervously.

Trying to redirect the conversation, Daphne said, "Wes, the paella was delicious. And, Raul, I want that recipe for the sangria, ok?"

Raul nodded, "Sure, Daphne, thanks."

I suggested, "Hey, looks like everyone's finished. Angelo, would you help me clean up the table? You guys can go by the pool and relax while we get dessert."

Getting dessert ready gave me the excuse to leave the table and go into the kitchen. Angelo followed me.

"Wes, man, does Matthew come with an instruction manual? How much longer to we have to put up with that ass? I think he was punched one too many times in the face," he said, referring to Matthew's short amateur boxing career. "Or maybe he was exposed to too much radiation at the power plant."

"Hey, it's almost over. Let's get through it." I was trying to be peacemaker, but I couldn't have agreed more with Angelo. But we both respected Clay too much to say anything.

"I know, I'll behave, but that guy needs to have the crap fucked out of him," Angelo said with a bit of aggression in his voice.

"He's not a bottom, remember?" I tried to get him to crack a smile.

"Yeah, that's his problem. He wants it but can't deal with playing a passive role." Angelo made a gesture with his finger, as if to say he'd like to give it to him and shut him up.

"Well, I asked Clay what was with Matthew this evening. He said he's had a rough time with family and is very depressed. I know it's not an excuse for his behavior, but I'm going to cut him a little slack the rest of the night and hope for the best."

Angelo nodded and conceded, "Okay, cool. I'll try to suck it up. And this Will character, I'm not sure about him. He's hot, but the dude seems like he's in another world."

I topped off a vodka gimlet that Angelo was nursing in the kitchen, hoping to mellow him out before going back to the table. He said he'd be cool.

Clay convinced Matthew to come back and join the rest of us outside for dessert. The remainder of the evening was more peaceful. Everyone was pretty laid out after a full dinner, dessert, and some serious drinking. Raul seemed content but as he relaxed his head on my shoulder I could tell he was relieved that dinner was over.

After we watched the sun drift low over the mountains, Clay and Matthew excused themselves and went to their room. Emil said his good-byes and went to his hotel, where he said he had advertised a "private party" in his room. Will thanked me for dinner, and he and Angelo went out the front door. Raul went to the kitchen to starting cleaning up.

I was bringing glasses in from outside when Angelo burst through the front door. Surprised at seeing him return, I asked, "Hey Angelo, what's up? I thought you and Will were going to hang out?"

Angelo's was steaming mad. Even his ears were bright red. "What a fucking asshole. We get outside and the prick says, 'Okay, it's two hundred dollars an hour, three hundred if it's anything goes.' He's a damn hustler. And when I told him hell no, he says, 'What about the lady inside, think she's interested?' I was so close to knocking his lights out. I just said the evening is over and turned away."

"Oh my God. I'm so sorry, man. I can't believe it. He told me was involved with the community. I had no idea how involved." I felt so bad that I had put Angelo in that position. We laughed about it months later, but we agreed: no more blind dates.

Angelo slapped me affectionately on the rear and retreated to his room.

I went into the kitchen and helped Raul finish cleaning up.

"Well, Raul, quite a cast of characters, isn't it? I hope you weren't too offended."

Raul, his head down while wiping the counters responded, "No, I am a pretty resilient guy. Most of your friends are great guys. It's obvious that Angelo thinks the world of you."

That comment struck me as a bit odd. Maybe I'm so close to Angelo that I wasn't aware, but was it that obvious that we were such close friends?

It was a long day. Raul and I crashed. We fooled around for a little while but soon fell asleep in one another's arms.

Come morning, everyone made their own breakfast and headed their respective ways. Clay and Matthew drove back to LA, and Raul went home to get ready for a business trip the following day. Angelo and Daphne stayed for another day. Daphne suggested going for a hike, thinking it would do us good to get out in the wilderness. I suggested the Mary Jane Falls trail on top of Mount Charleston. I was the tallest peak in southern Nevada and only a half-hour drive from the house. It was a three-hour round-trip hike to the falls that was full of switchbacks, but the scenery was gorgeous. Because of the nearly eight-thousand-foot altitude, the temperature was a good twenty degrees cooler than the desert floor. We found a nice spot to lay down a blanket and munch on some sausage, bread, and cheese that we'd packed. It was a beautiful view of the desert in the distance. We didn't have to say much. We were enjoying one another's company and the beautiful day. We were like an old pair of shoes: worn, but they fit just right.

When we were ready to leave, Angelo put his arm around me and gave me a kiss on the cheek. It was different from the other times that we hung out together and cuddled in the same bed. It was as if he was telegraphing something special that he was feeling that afternoon. I didn't have to ask because I was feeling the same thing.

I was sorry to see both of them leave for the airport the next day, but we agreed to get together again soon.

My first dinner in my new town was over. We all survived.

Eight:

꧂ ꧂ ꧂

Jesse

Earlier, at our dinner, Angelo had inquired about the handsome dude at Kevin's services. I knew he was speaking about Jesse. Even though Jesse was straight and married with children, we had gradually grown closer during Kevin's illness. I had told Angelo about him, especially what a sexy man he was, and that he seemed to be unusually friendly for a straight guy. Angelo cautioned me about getting involved with a married man, assuming, and rightly so, that I would love to have jumped in his pants.

I told Angelo several times, "Jesse and I are just friends. It's not like that." I had wondered if my nose was growing as I said that, knowing full well how much I'd love to get something on with Jesse. Even though just six months had passed since losing Kevin, I still needed sexual gratification, which was quite separate from any emotional adjustments that still challenged me.

Angelo couldn't believe that nothing happened between us when Jesse drove out to Vegas to help me move.

"Man, you had the perfect opportunity and you blew it, Bo," Angelo teased.

"No, I didn't blow it," I responded with a smile on my face.

"Yeah, wishful thinking I guess," Angelo said with a smirk.

Since the move, Jesse had started to call me every few weeks. At first I thought it was because he missed his friendship with Kevin and I was his connection to that memory. But lately, the calls had become less about Kevin and more about what was going on with me. The latest call was the boldest yet. Jesse wanted to come and visit and was already prepared to give me a date for when he'd like to come. I had no problem clearing my calendar for his visit. Something told me it would be special.

❖　❖　❖

I picked Jesse up at the airport. As I waited in baggage claim, he appeared on the escalator headed toward me. It had been a few months since I had seen him. He looked every bit as handsome and sexy as I remembered. He saw me and gave me a thumbs-up. His big grin was wide enough to make his eyes squint.

"Damn," I said to myself.

Jesse wrapped his arms around me and said, "Hey, DB, great to see ya, man." He wore a dark blue short sleeve shirt unbuttoned, exposing a white tank top that hugged his taut torso.

I could smell his deodorant as his arm raised on my shoulder. When he hugged me I could feel the patch of hair on his chin rub against my cheek.

I responded, "Welcome back to Sin City, J-Bones. How you been?"

Jesse answered as his arm pulled me closer into his chest. "I'm cool, and I'm so glad you let me hang with you. I need this."

We stopped and got some fried chicken on the way home.

As we pulled up the driveway, Jesse turned to me and put his hand on my shoulder. "DB, I really appreciate your letting me visit, man. I needed to get away and clear my head, and besides, it's great to see you. You're looking great—still workin' out I see." I could feel his hand squeeze my shoulder.

It was nice of him to thank me, but there was a hidden anxiety evident in his speech. I figured the "worry chest" would open once he had a drink and a toke.

◆　　◆　　◆

And how right I was. After lunch, I made us each a vodka and cranberry. Jesse had changed into his swim trunks and a tank top. We had a quick toast, and he gave me another big hug, one that again seemed to last uncomfortably long for a straight man. After all, this wasn't a boyfriend visiting me for a "good time" weekend.

Putting his hand under his tank top to rub his stomach Jesse said, "DB, let's hit the pool, okay?"

Jesse sat on the edge of the pool next to me. He sipped his drink and quietly said, "Ah, this is the life, man." His toned body, deeply tanned, made the tattoos he got years ago barely visible.

He stripped off his tank and trunks, revealing a brief blue speedo. He jumped in the pool and climbed onto the floating raft. He lay on his back and shut his eyes, as if waiting for the sun to cleanse him of all of his worries. I was surprised he said very little that afternoon, fully expecting him to start crying on my shoulder about something. He was enjoying the sun and water. I, in turn, was enjoying the sight of him in his speedo. For the first time, I got a glimpse of the generous package that all the ladies were gossiping about. The wet speedo outlined it in great detail. I felt self-conscious looking at him so often and found myself getting hard trying to imagine him kneeling over me.

An hour or two must have passed. I had fallen asleep on the

lounge under the Palo Verde tree. I felt a nudge on my arm. I opened my eyes to find Jesse standing over me wrapped in a towel. He handed me a fresh cocktail and sat down on the lounge next to me. Again, he put his arm on my shoulder, giving me a gentle squeeze with his strong hands.

"Hey, DB. This is what the doc ordered, you know? I love coming here. It's an escape for me." Little beads of water still clung to the curly patches of hair on his chest.

I said, "You're always welcome here, Jesse."

I took a sip of my drink and continued, "So, what's been going on with you, man? Everything cool at work?"

"Yeah, DB. Same ol'. Just glad to have a job, I guess. Maybe someday I won't have to struggle so, you know. I mean, look at you. You got everything." He shrugged his shoulders, probably having thought about me losing Kevin. Realizing he may have misspoke, he added, "Well, almost, I guess."

"I suppose we're never satisfied, eh, Jesse? All of us are on a continual search for something more. I'm trying to appreciate what I have and to not long for much more other than good health and a few good friends."

Jesse paused, and an unusually serious tone descended upon him. "Say, DB, you know—Naomi and I, well, we're havin' lots of problems."

Here it comes, I thought.

He nervously rubbed his hand over his short but thick black hair as if hoping a genie would appear and let him wish his problems away. "She don't understand me, and I guess I'm still havin' a hard time settling down. You know, it ain't easy being married after living like I was in a candy store all those years."

He obviously was referring to his frequent sexcapades with all the young ladies he'd meet at the strip club—a true "dog," he would admit. While he said he didn't dance or escort anymore, I suspected he would still sneak in a paying customer if the price was right.

"I know, Jesse. I imagine it's a big adjustment for you, but Naomi seems like a great lady. Relationships take effort. You just don't put a quarter in and out comes the prize. After all, you guys haven't been married for much more than a year, have you?"

Jesse replied, "No. I guess the responsibilities that come with it freak me out sometimes. It was Naomi's suggestion I come out to see you and clear my head. She's a cool lady."

Cool? I thought. *I don't know of too many women who would be so understanding.* Maybe she needed some time for herself as well. Naomi knew I was gay and probably felt safer with Jesse being with me more than anyone else.

With an almost guilty look on his face Jesse confessed, "DB, there's somethin' else. We're both seein' other people. It started with another couple down the street. We had 'em over for dinner, and we all had too much to drink. Before I knew it, we were all messin' 'round together."

Jesse shook his head and took a long sip on his drink. He continued, "Even though we never got together with 'em again, seems like it opened the door to other things. Funny, man, I always felt that I was the 'dog' that could fool around, but after seein' how Naomi got it on with another dude, man, I panicked. I can't even hold her anymore, let alone be intimate with her."

He hung his head as he wiped his eyes that started to fill with tears. "I'm really a fuck-up, aren't I, DB?"

"Have you guys thought of counseling? It might be worth it to try before you guys give up on one another," I suggested as I wrapped my arm around his shoulder.

A veil of worry overcame him. Jesse replied, "Maybe, DB, but listen, man, let's not talk anymore about it right now. I don't want to bring you down, and I just wanna get my drink on, okay?"

I felt bad for Jesse but was relieved that at the very least he was able to talk about it. I figured we'd resume the conversation later. I put on some CDs and turned the volume up on the outdoor speakers. Jesse stared off into space and rocked his head to the beat of the music. We spent the rest of the afternoon by the pool, refilling our glasses several times.

❖　❖　❖

Jesse wanted to cook me a nice dinner. He went to the store and got supplies. I made a drink for him while he cooked dinner. He grilled fish and veggies outside and prepared a fried rice dish that filled the kitchen with the smell of coconut, peanuts, and ginger. Jesse could cook his ass off. What woman, or man, wouldn't find him a great catch? I had to remind myself that he brought a lot of baggage with him, so that fantasy was short-lived.

After dinner, we sat out by the pool with a cocktail, watching the sun go behind the mountains. The balmy desert evenings were one of my favorite things about living there. As the dimming light of dusk arrived, the mountains ringing the city became awash in a purple veil, punctured only occasionally by distant snowy-white peaks. Once foreboding, the cool hues of the mountains were now more welcoming. The sunset vanished quickly but it was a special moment that didn't go unnoticed by Jesse. Neither one of us said anything. We didn't have to. The evening was a beautiful end to a day filled with the comfort and security of being home with the company of a good friend. As for Jesse, I'm sure similar thoughts were filling his mind. He glanced at me once and gave me that half wink indicating his approval and pleasure.

Jesse got up and made us each one more drink. We finished them off outside. It was dark, but the garden lights gave a resort-like feel to the yard. Again, we sat there without saying much. I think Jesse was reluctant to bring up his marital problems and risk ruining the atmosphere of a nice evening. Finally, I told him I was tired and that it was time to hit the sack. I made sure he had fresh towels in the guest room. He gave me another of his extended hugs and thanked me. I went to my room and soon fell asleep.

I don't think I was asleep for more than an hour when I thought I heard something moving. I was half-asleep. My first thought was that I was having that ugly dream again. Suddenly, a figure appeared standing over me.

"It's okay. It's me, Jesse," he whispered.

Nothing more was said. Jesse slipped out of his boxers, crawled into my bed, and without hesitation, cuddled up next to me. He turned me over so my back was nestled into his stomach. His muscled arms pulled me close. His warmth comforted me and I suddenly felt protected—from what, I didn't know. His manly scent overcame me as he pulled me tightly against him. It was as if he couldn't get close enough to me. I became aroused in seconds, quickly suspending my disbelief at what was happening. Holding me in his tight grasp, he slowly ground his hips. I could feel his stiff erection against me. Jesse suddenly pulled me over on top of him. We didn't kiss but his big brown eyes looked directly into mine and burned me up with a look of lust and desire. With a slight grin and nod, he indicated approval to pleasure him.

His large hands gently pulled my head into his chest. I could hear his heart beating rapidly. I followed the narrow line of short black curls that ran from the middle of his chest down his stomach. As I inhaled, I could smell his manly musk. I kissed and licked his stomach, which quickly became moist. The taste of his sweet and salty sweat filled my senses with a desire to explore him. He pushed my head down further. His scent grew stronger. I thought I was going to explode, but I let him stay in control. After all, I knew he was "straight" and needed to do this his way.

He groaned as I started to please him, and all the while his hands caressed and guided my head to where he wanted. It was over in minutes. He said nothing. We lay still. After a few minutes, our breathing had slowed back to a normal rate. I remained silent in disbelief, anticipating an awkward moment. Should I say anything? Was he going to trip and get angry like some straight guys would do in order to preserve their dominance and masculinity? My worries vanished when he pulled me back up and rolled me over so that my back again was facing him. He gave me a kiss on the top of my head, still not saying a word. With his arms wrapped around me, his warm breath on my neck was the last thing I remembered before falling asleep. I didn't hear him get up and go to his room.

When I woke up I could tell the sun was just coming up. There was an orange glow outside. I suddenly realized I was alone. Jesse was gone. That was probably good, since it would have been awkward waking up next to him. I smelled bacon and heard the coffee pot gurgling. As soon as I sat up, Jesse surprised me and came in the room with a hot cup of coffee.

Wearing only his boxers, he greeted me. "Good morning, DB. Breakfast will be ready soon." He went back to the kitchen, acting as if nothing happened. *Wow*, I thought. *Did something really happen?* I saw a small towel and washcloth next to me and realized, yeah, it had.

Jesse took a quick morning swim but said he needed to catch an afternoon flight back to LA. I was surprised he was leaving so soon, but he said he only had intended to get away for the day. He had to work that evening's night shift.

As we went out to the car for the ride to the airport, he came from behind, grabbed my shoulders and turned me around.

He looked straight into my eyes for what seemed like an eternity, and said, "DB, thanks. Life's complicated and sometimes, ya know, we don't need explanations for everything. You're the best. You're my soul brother. I love you, man."

I was surprised by how forthcoming he was and comfortable with what had happened between us the night before.

We didn't say much on the way to the airport. I dropped him off, and we agreed to talk soon. He nodded, grinned, and gave me that little wink that I'd seen the day before. I knew that whatever problems he arrived with were taking off on that plane with him. Perhaps our brief evening together had given him some degree of pleasure and comfort. I hoped so.

I drove back home, a restrained smile on my face. Gazing out the windshield at the pinkish mountains in the distance, I relived what had occurred only hours earlier. Jesse had come and gone, in more ways than one. I took his advice and decided not to search for explanations right now.

Nine:

⑾ ⑾ ⑾

Miami Reunion

It was time to start preparing for my business trip to Miami, followed by a reunion with my Ecuadorian friend, Tico. While I was excited to see Tico again, I was filled with apprehension regarding the troubles in which he seemed to find himself embroiled.

My conference was going to be easy since I was a passive participant and didn't have to make any presentations. It was as much an excuse for me to get away as it was a networking opportunity for work. Angelo had a gig in San Juan, Puerto Rico, and said he'd be able to spend the weekend in Miami with me.

The conference involved the usual conservationists, biologists, and political advocates that I had seen or met at similar meetings. Still, it was a good way to stay in circulation and keep current. Occasionally, I would meet someone new on the scene. After all, I had met Raul at a similar conference in Phoenix only a few months earlier. I was always amused and somewhat mystified about fate and destiny. I didn't believe in coincidence. Rather, it seemed to me that people's fates were intertwined for a reason, good or bad.

On the last night of the conference, I decided not to attend to the final dinner in order to meet up with Angelo. He arrived in Miami from San Juan late that afternoon and got a room at the same hotel for that one evening before heading back to San Juan. I had just showered and changed into some casual clothes when he texted me, "Hey, Bo, I'm at the bar lining up the vodka gimlets. Hurry before the olives get soggy." I messaged him back that I was on my way.

◆   ◆   ◆

I walked up to the hotel lobby bar. Angelo wasn't kidding. He had two vodka gimlets lined up on the bar.

As we embraced I smelled the sweet yet manly scent that was unique to Angelo.

Sporting a devilish grin he said, "Drink up, Wesley boy. I've got an evening planned for us."

His silky T-shirt clung to him, outlining the muscled body that he was still able to maintain while traveling with the band.

I teased him. "How do you manage to stay in such good shape, Nico? Chasing the boys?"

Loving the compliments, Angelo flexed his veiny bicep and put my hand around it.

"I stay strong by pushing them all away, see?" He laughed.

I playfully replied, "I'm impressed, Captain America, but let's finish these drinks so you can demonstrate your technique at the Warehouse. That place is still open, isn't it?"

"I don't know. It's been a long time since I've been on the town here." Angelo liked to joke around as though he was a "player," but in reality he was a homebody and oddly shy for a performer.

I asked, "How's the show going in Puerto Rico? Did you add some spicy salsa to your funk for the locals?"

Loving to talk about his music, he answered, "It's a great venue,

Wes. It's at one of the large hotels, so the clientele is mostly from the States and Europe. We added some Latin percussion to the band just for this show. It seems to be going over well."

With regret in my voice, I said, "You know, I should have planned an extra couple of days to go back to San Juan with you and see your show."

He nodded and replied, "Yeah, that would have been cool, but there'll be other shows."

I replied, "Yeah, but those island boys are sweet. Did you meet anyone interesting in SJ?"

Angelo gestured as though he'd put his finger on a hot stove. "Well, there was a guy in the audience who came to every show. This dude was built like a football player. He came backstage after one of the shows and seemed like a really nice guy. He came up to my room after one of the shows."

"Was it jumpin' jack or just flash?" It was our code for "hot with re-date possibilities" or just a "one time, flash-in-the-pan quickie."

"All flash, man. No breakfast." Angelo tried to force a chuckle, but he seemed bothered. "He had to rush off to get back to his wife. The story of my life, it seems." He got up off the stool and leaned on the bar rail. He stared at the bottles lined up behind the bar.

I was sorry I had brought up the subject.

Tapping him on the shoulder I said, "Well, let's get this night started, Nico. Your best buddy is here to enjoy the evening with you."

We left the hotel and went to a couple of dance bars that we both recalled from previous visits. Neither one of us had the expectation to trick out. We enjoyed one another's company and were content to leave it at that.

It was almost 3:00 a.m.—way past my bedtime. We took a taxi back to the hotel, soaking wet from a night of dancing in the hot humid Florida air and a little drunk. He was hanging on my shoulder as we walked through the lobby to the elevators. The few guests that were around took a glance at us, probably wondering what we were up to.

As the elevator stopped on my floor, Angelo whispered, "Nico, can I just come over to your room?" His silk shirt was soaking wet and sticking to his ripped body.

As soon as we got to the room we both stripped and climbed into bed. I noticed he wasn't wearing any underwear, which wasn't unusual for him.

I joked, "Still going commando after all these years?"

"Yep, makes doing the laundry easier," he replied with a wide grin.

We probably weren't in bed more than five minutes before we fell sound asleep, holding one another as we usually did when we crashed together. A sense of security swept over us when we were together and that seemed to trump any physical attraction we had to one another. We both restrained ourselves, knowing that what we had was special and not wanting things to change.

The next morning, we woke up later than I had planned, but it didn't matter. My flight to Quito wasn't until that evening, and Angelo had a late-afternoon flight to LA. We ordered room service for coffee and a leisurely breakfast.

Angelo sipped his coffee and said, "You know, Wes, I'm starting to get tired of traveling. It's great money, but I'm burned out." Angelo fiddled with the handle of his mug. "You can't really develop any relationships on the road, and I'm afraid of getting old and of being alone."

He stood up and stretched, and with his back to me he continued, "The other thing that bothers me is all the roadies and groupies that get obsessed with coming to the shows. It's flattering at first, but some of these folks are obsessed."

He took a bite of his croissant. "I had one lady break into the dressing room in the back and throw herself at me. Security came and got her, but you know they found a small pistol in her purse? Crazy, man."

"Damn, people are nuts," I commented. "I sort of figured the time would come when you'd say enough is enough." I tried not to display my selfish pleasure in hearing of his plans to settle down.

Angelo smiled. "You know, I've been wise with my money, at least, and have stashed enough away. Besides, I know I'm not a youngster anymore, and the good looks won't ..." He didn't finish. He sat down and looked away.

I moved my chair closer to his and put my arm around him. "You know, buddy, it's okay. Maybe it's time to make a drastic change. Hey, look at me. I'm surviving. It hasn't killed me yet."

Angelo's eyes got wet and he looked at me intently. "You miss Kevin a lot don't you, Wes?"

"Of course," I replied. I could see Kevin in my mind then, as if Angelo's simple comment had conjured up Kevin's face and smell and the strong feel of his hand in mine. "He will always be a part of me, but I know I have to move on. And I have so many good memories."

"That's good. That's good." Angelo nodded and stirred his coffee fast. The spoon rattled against the ceramic mug.

"Nico, have you ever really been in love? I mean crazy good love?" I leaned forward in my chair and looked at Angelo with my eyes fixed on his.

"Only once did I feel what it would be like to be in love," Angelo continued. "I didn't give it the chance to happen, though, and I've always regretted that." He closed his eyes and I could feel a sense of melancholy descend over him.

"When was that?" I asked.

Before Angelo could open his mouth to speak my phone buzzed with a text. It was the airline notifying me that my flight had been moved back one hour. Angelo took his mug off the table and walked away. His shoulders seemed stooped, his pace slow.

We never resumed the conversation.

Since he had an earlier flight and wanted to stop at a favorite Cuban bakery, he was going to leave as soon as he cleaned up and get a taxi. We said our goodbyes, both feeling a sense of sadness hanging in the air.

"Have a safe flight, Wes. Let's talk next week." He gave me a little kiss on the neck and left to go to his room to pack and shower.

I sat on the sofa and had another cup of coffee. The room filled up with a sense of loneliness. I started to contemplate the next part of my trip, which left me a bit anxious. I disliked the feeling of not being in control. Restless, I jumped in the shower, packed up my stuff, got a taxi and headed for the airport. I figured I could have a cocktail at the bar by the gate and get myself in the right frame of mind for Quito.

Ten:

〰 〰 〰

Journey to the Center of the Earth

I looked out the window as we were making our approach into Quito. Night landings were always nerve-racking, as there were volcanic peaks surrounding the city. Below, the lights of Quito were dim and concentrated in a very small area. Landing at ten thousand feet meant that the plane had to be flying at a higher speed to maintain its lift. We hit the runway with a bit of a jolt that would awaken any hard-core traveler, but at least we arrived safely.

After I got my bags, I put on my Spanish thinking cap. Although many in the hospitality industry spoke English, I knew I would be better off using my Spanish whenever possible. Besides, it was a good opportunity for me to brush up on my language skills.

I stayed at the Hotel Intercontinental in the new part of town. It brought back a wash of memories, as this was the hotel I first stayed in upon arriving years ago for my UN mission.

❖   ❖   ❖

Tico had left me the phone number of a friend with whom he was staying while he recuperated from his assault.

I responded to the greeting on the voice mail. "Hola, Tico. It's Wes. I just checked in the Intercontinental. Call me when you get this message."

My previous trips to Quito had always been pleasant, filled with anticipation and excitement. This time, I was anxious and felt a heavy burden of responsibility for Tico's welfare. Normally, I would have headed out to my old stomping grounds, but I decided to stay and have dinner in the hotel and a drink at the bar.

I was on my second vodka gimlet when my cell rang.

"Wes, it's Tico. Welcome back to Quito. Did you have a good trip?" His voice crackled with relief that I had arrived.

"Hey, Tico. Yeah, everything's fine. But what about you? How are you feeling?"

While he tried to be upbeat, I could tell there was a wavering in his voice. He wasn't quite himself yet.

"I'm much better now. I can actually see out of both eyes!" He was trying to joke but it only made me realize how badly he must have been beaten. "I've been crazy waiting for you to get here. A friend of mine, Gustavo, was a great help, but I need to get back to my life and business. I can take care of myself now."

"Good, should I come by in the morning?" I asked.

Tico replied, "Yeah, I'll text you the address. It's only about one kilometer from the hotel. How about 10:00 a.m.?"

"That's fine. See you then, chico."

"I'm really glad you're here, Wes. We have a lot to talk about." Tico's voice faded as he hung up.

I thought to myself, *I bet there is a lot to talk about, probably more than I want to know.* I ordered one more vodka gimlet. With the help of the altitude, the booze was starting to hit me hard. I finished up and headed to my room comfortably drunk. Incapable of too much worry, I slept like a rock.

◈   ◈   ◈

The alarm woke me up. I glanced over at the nightstand. The little travel alarm I brought read 9:00 a.m. Damn. I needed to shower, grab something to eat, and head over to Tico's. I ordered room service so I wouldn't have to wait in the restaurant. By the time I showered, my juice, fruit, and rolls were waiting by the door.

I decided to walk to Tico's place. It would give me a chance to get reacquainted with Quito—and to test my endurance in adjusting to the altitude. After walking two blocks, I was huffing and puffing, but it still felt good to be out in the Andean air. The low clouds seemed to scrape the landscape as they drifted by. As I walked past strangers, they would nod and say hello, a reminder of how friendly most Quiteños were. Showing little disdain or aloofness to strangers, the people of Quito loved to talk with foreigners, as though wanting to learn some great secrets from outside of Ecuador.

I made it to Tico's apartment after walking for about twenty minutes. It wouldn't have taken me that long if I hadn't stopped at the local market to look at all the local produce and meats. I still shuddered at the sight of guinea pigs, the local delicacy, hanging in the market.

Tico answered my knock on the door with a burst of energy.

"Hola, mi cielo." He hugged me much harder than I thought his small framed body could manage, and I could hear him groan in pain as I pressed against him. "Oh, Wes, I'm so glad you're here."

Tico's apartment was small and sparsely furnished. In two corners of the living room were stacks of CDs and flyers advertising the bar. The walls were bare except for one large tattered poster of the Supremes.

"Tico, it's great to see you, though you have looked better, my dear." His face was healing, but there were still stitches in his lower lip and a dark bruise over his left eye. "They really did a job on you, eh?" I was trying to be cheerful.

"Yep, I'm still a bit sore. I wish I could say I did some damage as well, but yeah, they got the best of me." He shook his head. "Wes, it was terrifying. I have never been so frightened."

Tico sat on the couch, propping his sore back up with pillows.

Even though we hadn't seen one another in quite a while, we talked often and routinely sent e-mails. It was easy to pick up where we left off.

Tico was half-dressed. I could see dark marks on his shoulders and back. I thought, *The guys who did this were serious.* My brief euphoria of being back in Quito evaporated. I started to feel anxious about the real reason I came back. I didn't want to end up lying half-dead in the jungle.

"How's your family doing? Do they know what happened to you?" I asked.

Tico tried to put on a strong front, but I could tell it still hurt when he smiled. "They're cool, enjoying retirement and trying to learn to play golf at ten thousand feet." He chuckled. "They don't know anything about this, Wes. I told them I had been on vacation to give my bruises time to heal up and fade away. There was no need to alarm them."

We looked at one another as if to say, "Okay, we'll have time to catch up later. Let's figure out how to get out of this jam."

I suggested, "Tico, let's go grab some coffee or something, okay?"

"Sure, there's a little café around the corner. We can celebrate your arrival with a beer and ceviche." Tico finished getting dressed.

I had forgotten about the tradition of beer and ceviche, or their version of a shrimp cocktail, to help fight hangovers.

While we enjoyed the ceviche, Tico started to explain the horror he experienced.

"The Diablos, or DCs, came back to the bar one night."

I recalled the time years ago when we were alone in his bar and a questionable-looking character came through the back door and spent a few minutes in the back room with Tico. I imagined he had been paying them off ever since.

"They wanted their usual payment for what they called "protection." Yeah, some protection! They extorted a lot of the business on the street. I told them I didn't have the money this month." Tico took a long sip on his beer.

He continued, "That was partly true, since it was a very slow month for business. I did have an emergency fund stashed away, but I didn't want to use that. I thought I could buy some time. Well, they weren't willing to negotiate."

Tico's voice trembled as he recounted what happened next.

"One night after I had closed the bar, they abducted me, tied to the back seat of a jeep, and drove me out into the jungle. I was blindfolded, so I didn't even get a good look at them, let alone where they were taking me." Tico paused and exhaled. It was as if he was experiencing the abduction all over again.

"Before I knew it, I was laying on the ground while they kicked and punched me. I must have passed out, because when I woke up it was daylight. All I remember is that before I passed out, they kept saying this was only a warning. 'Settle up or you're dead.'"

Tico spun the beer bottle around in a nervous gesture.

"I made my way back to a main road where a farmer picked me up and dropped me off at a hospital. The doctors wanted to call the police but I lied and told them that I just got drunk and got into a fight at a bar. If I had told them the Diablos were involved, I'd surely be beaten again."

I moved my chair close to him and put my arm around him as he finished recounting his story.

"Anyway, I have until the end of this month to settle up or they will come to finish the job. I owe them five hundred dollars. That's a lot of money here, Wes. "

I responded, "That's a lot of money anywhere, Tico. So, what do you know about these guys, the Diablos? Are you sure it wouldn't be better to just call the police and let them handle it?" After I suggested that, I realized how silly that probably sounded to Tico. Police in Ecuador and many other South American countries were corrupt.

"Oh, listen, the police don't care, and some of them probably have ties to the DCs. And don't worry, Wes, the DCs aren't like the drug cartels. They're just a local gang of thugs."

"Don't worry? They nearly killed you!" I exclaimed. The thought that they were just local hoodlums looking for some notoriety didn't provide me any comfort.

"It'll be okay, trust me. We can handle this. If I get the police involved, the gang will only look for retribution and I'll be in even more danger."

I was about to question my own sanity for even thinking about meeting face-to-face with these gang members.

I told Tico, "Okay, on one condition. After we pay them off, you need to promise to close the bar and walk away. I know it's your baby, but it doesn't seem like things will change." Tico was nodding in agreement as I spoke.

"These guys will just come back in a month, and you'll be back in the same situation. Promise me, Tico?"

"Yeah, I'm ready to give it up, Wes. I just wish I could recoup my investment, as small as it is." Tico's expression showed both relief and disappointment.

"Well, when are you supposed to meet with these guys? Do they know that I'm coming?"

He explained, "I told them a friend is helping me get the money. I just have to contact them and set up a date."

"OK, I can help you with the money, but you need to do the talking," I insisted.

We went back to his apartment. He was tired from the meds he was still taking and wanted to rest. I told him we can get together tomorrow. In the meantime he was going to try to contact one of the Diablos and set up a meeting.

I gave him a gentle hug and agreed to talk first thing in the morning.

I walked back to the hotel and stopped at the lobby bar. I couldn't believe I was about to start negotiations with gang members in a foreign country. My only assurance was that I still carried a diplomatic passport from my work with the UN. Even though it had expired when I left the UN project, I brought it with me anticipating that if I flashed it to the Diablos they might think twice about doing anything to me. The idea that I could grant myself some degree of immunity was probably naive, but I figured it couldn't hurt.

❖   ❖   ❖

It was about 10:00 p.m. Tico closed El Barcito early, telling the few patrons present that he had repairs to do. After they all left, he locked the front and back doors and turned off the music so he could hear if someone knocked on the door.

I asked Tico to pour me a scotch. I wanted to be clearheaded when meeting these guys but needed something to calm my nerves. I was just about to take a sip when there was a loud knock on the rear door. I think I must have jumped several inches off the bar stool. Tico and I glanced at one another as if to say, *This is it, pal. Let's make it work.*

Tico unlocked the back door. To my surprise, the three young men who entered the bar were all well dressed in slacks and short-sleeved polo shirts. The first two quickly glanced around the small bar, making sure we were alone. The last one to enter was obviously the leader. He was dressed similarly but wore a brimmed hat. All of them sported the same tattoo on their left forearm: the letters "DC" topped with a jagged line to resemble the Andes. Their tattooed insignia, I thought, looked more like a logo for a trendy outerwear company than a Colombian gang of thugs. Given their relatively clean-cut dress, I wondered if these guys were really members of a tough gang. But when the leader started to speak, I realized they meant business.

The leader, who only spoke Spanish, first spoke to Tico and pointed to me.

"Is he the one?" His sharp glare pierced the artificial vale of confidence that I wore.

Tico simply said, "Yes."

All three looked at me with suspicion. I had hoped that the fear that was tearing up my stomach wasn't obvious.

Tico handed the leader the envelope with the five hundred dollars inside. He gave it to one of his lieutenants who quickly counted it and nodded that it was all there. Without saying any more, all three exited out the back door. It was over. I was relieved but stunned that it all happened so quickly, without any discussion or commotion.

Tico turned to me, "We need to get out of here, Wes. We shouldn't be here anymore."

I didn't question Tico's desire to leave right away, and he obviously didn't want to talk about the transaction. I was happy to oblige.

Tico hurriedly turned out the lights. As we exited through the front door, he paused and turned around, glancing back toward the bar.

I put my hand on his shoulder and said, "Tico, are you okay?"

He locked the door and turned around. He was dazed and could barely speak. "Not really, Wes. This was my life for the past fifteen years."

I took Tico back to the hotel where we sat at the bar for a while. I lost count of the number of drinks we had, but it was enough to where we were both feeling no pain. Tico seemed more at ease.

I said, "Tico, I'm surprised I was at how un-gang-like the Diablos were dressed."

With a sheepish grin, Tico replied, "Well, I had told them when I was setting up the meeting that I'd be accompanied by a diplomat from the United Nations to ensure my safety."

"No, you didn't!" I yelled so loud that other people in the bar looked at us.

Tico added, "I didn't know if they'd buy it, but apparently they were uncertain enough to be on good behavior. I guess even thugs dress up for an interview." We both started to laugh.

It was 2:00 a.m. The hotel bar had closed at 1:30 a.m. We just lingered to finish our last round. I told Tico I'd walk him back to his apartment. I was under the false illusion that there was still very little street crime in Quito, so I felt comfortable being out so late, despite the irony of having just negotiated with gang members.

We were about a block from the hotel when we noticed smoke at the end of the next block, toward where the bar was located. As we got closer, Tico yelled, "Oh my God!" He started running. El Barcito was engulfed in flames. The fire trucks had just arrived.

Tico grabbed my arm. "It really is over now, Wes." He rested his head on my arm.

Tico had suspected what the DCs were going to do after we left the bar that night. I understood then why he wanted to leave so quickly.

Tears ran down his cheeks. I rubbed the back of his neck to comfort him. "You'll be okay, Tico. It's time to move on."

"I know, Wes. I know." Tico stood there frozen, watching the bar disappear in the flames and smoke.

We walked slowly back to his apartment without saying much more.

The night air was fresh and cool. The sky was cloudless and the moon drifted behind the Pichincha volcano that watched over the city. Any other night this setting would have inspired love and romance. Tonight it provided comfort and relief. We said our good-byes for the evening.

Tico and I spent the following day just hanging out. Before I left, I asked him if he had seen Nareem, the guy I dated for a while when living in Quito. Tico said he still came to the capital every so often. I wrote down my address, phone number, and e-mail address and asked Tico to give it to Nareem if he saw him. While I doubted he had easy access to a computer, I hoped he would at least write. Tico said he would keep an eye out for him and pass on my information if he saw him. My memories of Nareem were still vivid, and I never dismissed the thought that we would someday meet again.

My flight back was later that evening. I offered to stay another day or two, but Tico said he'd be fine.

I invited him to come to Las Vegas when he got a chance. The change of scenery would've done him good. He promised me he would think about it.

Eleven:

꒑ꞏ ꒑ꞏ ꒑ꞏ

Am I Home Yet?

I t was great to see Angelo in Miami, but the Quito adventure drained me.

As the taxi pulled up the driveway, I felt a sensation I hadn't felt since living in Vegas. Despite having lived there less than a year, my house seemingly embraced me as I walked through the front door. My eyes actually got watery at the prospect that I had finally found some level of acceptance of my new life here. The jazz festival pictures on the wall that Kevin and I had acquired, which in recent months had been like painful daggers from the past, were now comforting reminders of the rich life I had enjoyed, that I had loved and been loved. Walking out to the back patio, I glanced across the landscape of desert plants. The different textures and blooms of the cacti and yuccas seemed to celebrate something beautiful, peaceful, and right. I still felt damaged, but I was home.

❖   ❖   ❖

I quickly went through my mail, which the neighbor had dropped off. A small envelope caught my eye. On the back was a wax seal. I knew it was from Clay and Matthew. They usually sent a thank-you note after every function. I peeled off the seal and slid out the small note inside:

Hey, Wes … Just a note to thank you for the dinner. It was great to see everyone as usual. Hope your trip went well. Will talk more soon. P.S. Matthew moved out again. Don't know if it's final this time or not. Headed to D.C. for Black Gay Conference. Love, Clay

I wasn't totally surprised, as I had heard this drill before. I knew Clay and I would be talking soon, but I was tired and not receptive to hearing more about other people's problems.

I had just finished reading Clay's note when Angelo sent me a text. "Welcome home Bo. Have been thinking about you. Hope you survived your Indiana Jones adventure…lol. See you soon, love Nico."

A warm feeling came over me when I read his text. It was both reassuring and comforting to know that someone like Angelo had your back. Even though LA was a stone's throw from Vegas, there were times I wished he lived closer. I guess it didn't matter, since he was on the road a good part of the time, anyway.

I put my suitcase in the bedroom, took a cold beer out of the fridge, and ordered Thai take-out. After I finished dinner, I got another beer and went on the patio. It was nearly dusk. The sky was full of pinks and oranges, and the mountains were cloaked in the usual purple haze. I was so glad to be home. I started to reflect on all that had happened in Quito. I wondered if I was crazy to have injected myself into Tico's problems. I put my life at risk in a part of the world where people disappeared without a trace. The morning I left Quito, I was awakened by a nightmare of being abducted by gang members and driven through the darkness of the Colombian jungle. The dream was so vivid that I had to call Tico to make sure he was okay. I was relieved when he picked up the phone and said he was fine. That nightmare was to recur, haunting me for months afterward. I dozed off on the chaise lounge on the patio. When I woke up it was 2:00 a.m. I staggered into the house and fell into bed.

❖　　❖　　❖

In my haste to get in the house after arriving from the airport the evening before, I failed to notice a note lying on the bench next to the front door. It was from Jesse. He was at a nearby hotel and needed to see me as soon as possible.

Fortunately, I had planned to take a couple of days off knowing that I'd be tired from the trip. I called Jesse at his hotel. When he answered, I didn't recognize his voice.

"DB, so glad you're back. Can I come over? It's urgent, man." His speech was so rapid that I could barely understand him.

I said, "Sure, of course." I No sooner was I home than another drama had unfolded.

"Cool, I'll take a taxi right over." He hung up.

I immediately assumed it was marital problems. It was, but there was something more.

❖　　❖　　❖

It seemed as though I had barely hung up the phone when a taxi pulled up to the house. Jesse must have had one idling in front of the hotel for him. He walked up to me and gave me his big bear hug. He looked his usual sexy self, but his head was down and he lacked his usual swagger.

We went into the house and I made him his favorite cranberry and vodka, and I made it stronger than usual. He asked how my trip was. I said "okay" but didn't feel like elaborating.

"So, Jesse, when did you get in town, yesterday?" I asked.

Jesse fidgeted while he spoke. "Yeah, I knew you were coming back home this weekend, and figured I'd just wait it out. Hey, I'm so sorry, man. I didn't want to lay any negative shit on you, man, but I thought I was goin' crazy and I had nobody to talk to. I felt like offing myself, to tell you the truth."

"Jesse, nothing can be that bad. Talk to me. What's going on? Is it Naomi? You guys still separated?"

He paused and took a long sip of his drink. "Yeah, we're still doing our own thing. I've adjusted to that mess, Wes. It's somethin' else now."

There was a painful pause.

"I got HIV, Wes. I got HIV." Jesse leaned over and grabbed me and started sobbing.

I held him for a few minutes without either of us saying anything.

"Hey, man, I'm here for you. A lot of people have HIV and live productive lives. It's not a death sentence." I tried to sound reassuring.

I knew my words were ringing hollow. But he needed a shoulder to cry on.

We talked for hours that night. Jesse broke down several more times. When we finally seemed to have exhausted our discussion, he acknowledged that he felt a little better and at least wasn't in a panic any longer. The news of being HIV positive was difficult for anyone, and it impacted everyone in different ways. For him, being straight (allegedly) and married (although now separated), it was very confusing. He felt a gay stigma attached to it and, of course, wondered about Naomi. Did he get it from her? Could he have given it to her?

I told Jesse he could stay as long as he wanted as long as he left here with a plan on what to do in terms of managing his health and how he planned to talk to Naomi about it. He agreed.

That night Jesse didn't even ask. He just came right in my bedroom, stripped down to his shorts, and got in bed with me. Nothing was said the rest of the night. We cuddled. There was no indication that he wanted or expected anything resembling the brief sexual encounter we shared a couple of months earlier. We slept.

When I woke up, Jesse was frying bacon and eggs for my breakfast. He knew I had to be at work early. For a guy who relished the "player" role, he had a sweet and gentle side that was endearing. He said he was just going to lounge by the pool and nap the rest of the day. He needed to take a break from "thinking," he said.

Jesse spent three days with me, each day pretty much the same. We cuddled at night, and he made me breakfast in the morning and had dinner ready when I got home. Damn, I almost felt married again!

Before he left, I helped him come up with several things he needed to do to take control of his situation. I referred him to my physician and medical group in LA who were experienced with HIV and AIDS patients. I also gave him contacts where he could get counseling. I immediately thought of Clay and sent him an e-mail asking if he would be willing to talk with Jesse and share the challenges and successes of his own struggle with HIV. I talked with Jesse about what seemed obvious to me, namely, safe sex practices. I was surprised how naive he was. He agreed that he needed to talk with Naomi. I also made him promise that we would talk at least twice a week. We agreed on a schedule where we'd both make ourselves available. I felt this was important, not only for his emotional stability, but I wanted to know how he was doing.

It broke my heart to send him home that day. When we parted at the airport, my eyes were getting watery.

"Jesse," I said, "I love you. You will be okay. I am here for you whenever you need to call, okay?"

Unable to speak, he nodded. His once-strong body seemed weak as he embraced me. Gone, at least for now, was the bravado that once powered his electric persona. While I knew he felt better now than on the day he arrived, I could see the fear in his face: he was about to go back and face a scary reality alone.

He walked toward the gate, his shoulders slumped, heavy with a burden he didn't yet totally understand.

Twelve:

⑂ ⑂ ⑂

Colombia—Forgive and Forget

M y job with the BLM was going well. At least that part of my life was fulfilling. I was glad to have found something to anchor me and bring me some degree of stability. But there were times when I wondered if I had made the right decision when I moved out to the desert. Maybe I was impatient. After all, most every aspect of my life had recently changed, and the lives of those around me didn't stand still either.

So often the go-to guy for friends and family in personal crisis, I believed in karma, that what you put out comes back to you at some point in time. The universe took care of those who contributed more positive energy than they used, and I had hoped that my balance sheet was in the plus column. Right or wrong, this philosophy had guided me for most of my adulthood and had served me well. Little did I know how soon I'd once again be tested.

❖   ❖   ❖

Raul went back to Columbia for three months to check on the construction of his home, and he invited me to visit for a couple of weeks. He planned to move back the following year after finishing his project in Las Vegas. He hinted that his house, being built in the middle of an old coffee plantation, would be a quiet and peaceful place for a couple to retire. Though a hopeless romantic, I was certainly reluctant to return to South America so quickly, since it had only been two months since the drama in Quito. But I did find the idea of visiting a native Colombian in his own country tempting, especially since I wouldn't be alone.

I had a lot on my plate at the BLM as I was responsible for designing an entirely new planning methodology suited to their bureaucratic environment. I wondered whether I could afford two weeks away, but I convinced myself I could work on the project while in Colombia. Since I had seen most of the major tourist sites in Colombia, I'd be spending most of the time relaxing in the countryside at Raul's house and could do some work from there. Though a very logical person most of the time, I was effective at rationalizing something that I wanted, even if it wasn't totally rational. Prior to my trip, I went to the doctor for my routine physical and tests. Fortunately, I got a clean bill of health.

❖   ❖   ❖

I planned to be gone a little over two weeks and already a week had passed. Raul's house was a romantic hideaway, just as he described. It was a three-story structure sitting on a knoll overlooking an old coffee plantation. He had leased the acreage to local farmers. There were banana trees surrounding the house on three sides. He had several workers who usually hung around the property. I'm not sure what their jobs were. They were young guys, and they seemed to be very interested in my arrival. I just figured I was something of a curiosity to them. I'd say a quick hello when I would encounter them. They would simply tap their caps in response.

The living areas were on the second and third levels. Typical of the construction in the area, the house was elevated by pillars, offering protection from heavy rains and wildlife. The ceilings were bamboo and the floors of a local wood similar to mahogany. It had the feeling of a tree house. It also afforded a stunning view of the surrounding plantation, which disappeared into a valley below, framed by forest-covered mountains on all sides. The second floor, or main area, had a bedroom, bath, modest kitchen, and open living area with a long balcony stretching the width of the house. The third and top level hosted a large loft and balcony. We slept in the loft. At night, the heavy tropical showers pounded on the tin roof. It was mesmerizing to hear the *ping pang* of big raindrops on the tin with the swish of rushing water spilling off the roof. I spent the early mornings sipping fresh Colombian coffee while sitting on the third floor balcony. I'd watch the fog retreat from the valley floor, revealing the snow-capped Andes in the distance. I was like living a fairy tale.

There was a television, but it only pulled in two channels, limiting its options to either soccer games or *novelas*. I opted for spending as much time outside as possible, usually talking with the farm hands tending to the coffee plants.

"Spend a little more time with the *vaqueros*, Beto, and I'll hire you as a ranch hand." Raul would chuckle at my fascination with the Colombian countryside, which he took for granted.

Some afternoons we'd take long walks through the coffee fields. The leaves of the plants glistened from the frequent showers. We'd occasionally cross paths with one of the workers out in the fields. They would carry satchels of fruits, including bananas, mangos, and papayas, to snack on while working. They would see us walking and offer us a handful of fruit to snack on. Perhaps this was Raul's plan all along, to let the gorgeous countryside and lush greenery seduce me first. Indeed, I found myself becoming infatuated with everything, and it took every bit of self-control to resist sending an email to the BLM that I was ending my short career with them. Raul was a loving, caring, and unselfish man, particularly in bed. I thought, *Damn, was there anything missing in the picture?* He pressed all of my physical buttons, but I still felt restraint in giving in emotionally.

There were moments when I imagined us together as a couple. We were attracted to one another. We were both bilingual. We had good careers and shared many of the same interests. But I felt I wasn't ready to start over and make that commitment. I was just getting my feet back on the ground and reestablishing my life in Las Vegas. Still, I knew that by not leaving myself open to another long-term relationship, I could be missing an opportunity to be with a wonderful, loving person.

Colombia's reputation for drug cartel wars and gang battles with government sympathizers was never lost on me. I was somewhat concerned, but Raul had reassured me before coming that gang violence had greatly reduced and that the government had regained control. Sure, cartels and drug traffic were still prevalent in Colombia, but the activities had gone underground. Raul said there was little threat to the civilian population and tourists. His reassurances quickly came to question one morning while I was having my coffee and reading the local paper. On the back page, I noticed a small news story about a youth gang that was extorting local businessmen under to premise of providing "protection." While not believed to be involved in drug trafficking, the gang was gaining prominence throughout Colombia. It was the next part of the story that made me feel most uneasy. It went on to say that in recent weeks the gang had abducted two foreign businessmen who had invested in an emerald mining operation in the Andes outside of Bogota. One of the businessmen was found executed in the jungle, and the other had been severely beaten. The name of the gang was the Diablos de la Cordillera, or DCs. I jumped up, my legs almost scalded by the hot coffee that splashed out of the mug. I debated whether to ask Raul about the story in the paper, but I opted to wait, preferring not to tarnish the perfect time we were sharing.

❖　　❖　　❖

From the house, it was a two-and-a-half-hour drive from the highlands to Santa Marta, a resort town on the Caribbean coast. Twice we made that trip to have dinner at one of the quiet beachside restaurants and then spent the night at a small local hotel. Santa Marta wasn't a great tourist destination for foreigners. Rather, it catered primarily to Colombians on holiday. This made it more appealing, as the streets weren't filled with T-shirt and souvenir shops whose owners anxiously awaited the arrival of the next cruise ship and its ensuing herd of passengers.

Like Ecuador but to a lesser extent, there was a dramatic change in the people, culture, and landscape as you descended from the plateaus of the Andes down to the coast. The people of the highlands were a mix of Spanish and more passive Indian cultures. Cuisine included some meats, potatoes, and maize. As you descended to the more tropical coastal areas, the population reflected African ancestry. The landscape was lush, and the food reflected the Caribbean diet of rice, beans, yucca, and fish.

Santa Marta was a small town, and Raul seemed to know everyone, shop owners and local officials alike. I even noticed younger, scruffier-looking guys, who gave the appearance of not having much to do, acknowledge Raul. He would just nod or wave, and the guys seemed satisfied that they were noticed.

Raul's favorite place to eat was a rustic beachside bistro on the outskirts of Santa Marta called La Conchita. It was a casual place and very unassuming from the outside. There were no buildings on either side of it for at least a block. It seemed to sit all alone on the beach, making you wonder if it was even open for business. After you entered, you were immediately swept into a different state of mind. The ceiling was thatch from coconut palms, the floor made of old wood planks, worn by many years of customer traffic. There was a small bar in the corner with four stools. The front had end-to-end folding doors that would accordion back to the sides of the restaurant, leaving the entire front open to the ocean and beach. While there were several small tables inside, most of the dining was outside on a crude stone patio. Each of the six wooden tables had an umbrella with a small hurricane lamp hanging from the inside. As the sun set, the waiter lit each hurricane lamp, resulting in a very romantic atmosphere. The sound of the surf barely drowned out the soft music coming from inside the restaurant. The menu was simple, mostly fish and mussels caught locally. The catch was posted on a chalkboard. Even though there was a bar, the drinks were limited to local beer and several hard liquors. We each had an Aguila, the local beer. Raul ordered the ceviche and a local fish called *mojarra*. For dessert we shared a *salpicón de frutas*, which was like a fruit cocktail made with watermelon juice and a dollop of ice cream on the top.

I started to feel that I was being romanced from the moment we entered La Conchita. The setting, the food, and the sexy Colombian were the perfect ingredients to serve up an evening that was both enchanting and seductive. Being the incurable romantic that I was, I knew I had the propensity to fall in love, but I questioned whether I still had the capacity to follow through. The downside of being a romantic was that it could lead you to places you're not ready to go. My resistance was weakening.

That evening we talked about life and former loves, and we cautiously avoided mentioning one another by name while describing future goals and desires.

Raul leaned back in his chair and looked out over the ocean panorama. He said, "Beto, my life has been hard. I've had to deny myself many things in order to survive." His eyes were intense as they focused on the horizon. "I've watched as others took time to enjoy life and, if lucky enough, have someone to enjoy it with."

I remained still and listened.

He continued, "I've been making a lot of decisions lately, making a lot of changes in my life. This time I'm doing things for me. Is that selfish?"

I paused for a moment and shook my head. "No, Raul, it's not."

Raul continued, "I want to move back to Colombia. My childhood here was painful and troublesome. There were things I'm not proud of. I know things will be different now, but sometimes it's hard to disengage from the past."

I reached across the table and cupped one of his hands in mine. "It's not selfish to follow your dreams, but there is a cost to everything."

The conversation reminded me of the very journey I was still undertaking.

I added, "As far as the past is concerned, you have to reconcile with whatever demons still follow you. This may be your greatest challenge, but you'll be free once you do."

Raul leaned back over the table, his head down but his eyes looking up at me. "Beto, I know you are right. Sometimes I get scared, and I never used to be that way."

There was no one left in the restaurant, so Raul pulled his chair closer to mine and put his arm on the back on my chair. He leaned over and kissed me on the ear. We sat there in silence and watched the lights flicker from the ships far out at sea.

Our voids in conversation weren't awkward as they could be on a typical date, but this date was anything but typical. Rather, they provided quiet breaks for both of us to enjoy the moment. Raul would look at me, his eyes soft yet intense. His lips moved slightly as if to invite me in. Was I falling for him, or just falling forward once again? I decided I wasn't going to worry about it that evening. I was going to follow my instincts and satisfy my own desire for romance and intimacy.

After dinner, we walked down the almost-deserted highway to our hotel. Our small room had sliding doors opening to the ocean. The sound of surf was gentle but constant. We were drunk, and both of us were aroused by one another's physical presence. We slept little that night, temporarily dozing off after an hour or two of making love. The lingering scent of our spent passion hung in the moist, tropical air and grew more intense through the night. It inspired us to further explore our fantasies and follow our instinctual drive to satisfy and be satisfied. Thankfully, we were out in the country where no one could hear us. I remember waking up that next morning, smelling fresh coffee that Raul brought up from the lobby. We sat on the balcony watching the fishing boats disappear on the horizon.

The next day we made the drive home back up to the highlands. We slept a good part of the next day.

That evening just around sunset, Raul grabbed me and said, "Come with me. I want to show you something."

We hiked up a hill behind his house. Near the top, Raul stopped and slowly waved his arm from left to right, as though he was blessing the acres of coffee fields before use.

With arms still outstretched, he said, "Beto, this could be ours together." While we had grown much closer the past week, I was still taken back by the implications of what he was offering. I wasn't able to respond right away.

He noticed and said, "Please, you don't have to say anything right now."

At that moment, he pulled a small parcel out of his pocket. It was wrapped in what appeared to be a small, worn canvas satchel.

He grabbed my arm and placed the satchel in my hand, and without letting go, he said, "Beto, I don't have great wealth, fancy cars, or a huge home. I do have an undying sense of loyalty and devotion to the person I love, and I love you. This is a simple symbol of how deeply I want to share my life with you. It's the original key of the coffee bean roasting house that my great-grandfather built. It sits right over there, over a hundred years old. Although it's no longer in use, this key is a cherished symbol of my family heritage. I offer it as a token of my love for you."

I slowly opened the satchel, being careful not to damage the deteriorating canvas. I reached inside and pulled out a key, about five inches long, made of thick iron that was worn and rusted. It was heavy for its size. On the handle were the engraved letters "VV" and the numbers "1898." Raul explained the initials indicated the name of the original ranchito, Vista Vallejo.

I held the key for a minute, again not knowing how to respond. I started to say, "Raul, this is …" He put his finger over my lips to signal me not to answer.

We sat on the hilltop awhile longer, watching the clouds drift lower and eventually conceal the distant mountaintops. As night fell, we walked back to the house and cooked dinner. I went to bed that night without giving him an answer to his proposal. After he fell asleep, I got up and sat out on the balcony for a while. I stared at the coffee fields, their shiny plants reflecting the bright moonlight. One thought kept running through my head: if this was paradise, could it last? I didn't realize at that moment how prophetic those thoughts would be.

❖   ❖   ❖

It was in the middle of the second week in paradise. I still hadn't found anything that was missing from what appeared to be a perfect world.

But I soon discovered some new information that swept through and flattened my idea of paradise like a hurricane storm surge.

Raul was in a rush that morning. He was late for meeting with a farmer in town who was going to take care of his acreage on a permanent basis. He got dressed in a hurry and headed downstairs to his car, yelling back that he'd be back by the early afternoon. Twenty minutes later, the house phone rang. Raul told me to answer while he was gone in case the farmer he was seeing had changed his plans. I answered the phone. It was Raul. He said in the rush to leave he forgot the address of the home where he was going to meet the farmer. He said it should be on a piece of paper on his desk.

While holding the phone in one hand I started to page through his messy desk with the other. "Is his name Felix Quintero?" I asked.

"Yes, what's his address?" I read off the address to Raul, and he told me he'd see me later. As I hung up the phone, I couldn't help looking down once again at his desk. Sticking out from beneath the papers was a photo. I gently pulled it out from the pile. It was a photo of Raul, looking a lot younger and sporting a tank top and a full head of short, black hair. What caught my attention was a tattoo on his left shoulder. It was the "DC" of the Diablos. My heart froze. It must have been the tattoo he had removed. I looked down again into the pile of papers on his desk. I would never have thought of violating his privacy and looking through his things, but, numb from disbelief, I irrationally waived his right to privacy and started thumbing through some of his papers. One particular paper caught my eye, perhaps because it contained a handwritten note written with a thick felt pen. I felt sick to my stomach. My shock turned to anger as I read the note.

Translated to English, it was addressed to "Jefe Caliche." *Caliche* was a term used to describe the hard cement like strata of sand and clay found just under the layer of topsoil. Raul once told me that he had a nickname given to him when he was a teenager that reflected his toughness and fearlessness. The note read, "Monthly meeting—Taverna Marcos, 9/14, 3pm. We'll expect you, Jefe." The note itself seemed innocent enough. It was the hand drawn symbol at the bottom of the note that sent a chill though my entire body. Again, it was the symbol of the Diablos gang. And they addressed him as *Jefe*, Chief? My God, I was sleeping with one of the leaders of the very gang that had terrorized Tico in Quito and me in my nightmares. How could I have been so deceived, so naive, and so careless? My hands trembled from anger and fear. I ran upstairs, pulled my suitcase out of the closet, and threw together the few belongings I had with me. Fortunately, I had already showered. I started the short walk to the local village for a taxi, figuring I would head to the airport and get whatever flight was available. Whether a rational move or not, I felt I had to leave right away. Any other time I probably would have waited and asked Raul about it. But given his connection with the same thugs that beat my friend Tico in Quito, I didn't want to wait for an explanation. After all, I wasn't exactly in neutral territory to have a major argument with a probable gang leader.

What compounded my anger was that I had told Raul all about Tico's problems in Quito and my subsequent trip there to help clear things up. The bastard had known the whole time. I wasn't sure whether to leave him a note explaining why I was leaving. Instead, I just took the piece of paper with the note about the meeting and left it lying on the bed upstairs. No further explanation would be necessary.

I was soaking wet by the time I got to the village, not so much from the warm, humid morning, but from the anger that was percolating inside me. While waiting at the taxi stand, which was beneath an old colonial style hotel, I saw two young guys, one in fatigues, the other in cargo shorts and a tank top. Their eyes seemed to follow me as I walked down to the corner where the taxis were lined up. Maybe my creative imagination was overactive after reading local news stories, but I felt fearful for the first time during my stay in Colombia. *Boy,* I thought, *wouldn't Matthew have had a field day with this, given his previous rant about gangs and South America?* I quickly jumped into the next waiting taxi, relieved that I had made it that far without Raul discovering that I had fled. As the driver took off in the direction of the airport, I noticed that the two suspicious men who were staring at me back at the taxi stand had gotten into a car that made a U-turn and began to follow. The one-hour ride to the Baranquilla International Airport seemed to take forever, and all the while, I expected the guys in the car behind me to pull up, force the taxi to the side of the road, and abduct me.

The men in the car followed the taxi for about twenty minutes, made a U-turn toward town, and disappeared. I felt incredible relief as we approached the airport. The next flight to Miami was in less than two hours. I paid a dear price to get on that flight. The *mordita,* or bite, was a typical requirement in many Latin countries to get what you want. The bribe I had to pay was well worth getting home. I was hoping Raul still hadn't returned from his meeting. I feared him seeing the note, driving to the airport, and making a scene. I went into the men's room, took a fresh shirt out of my luggage, wrapped the soiled one in a ball, and buried it in the suitcase. I rushed to security and customs, and after a surprisingly easy and uneventful document review, I headed to the gate. I heard the first boarding announcement for my flight. I wouldn't worry about getting a flight to Las Vegas until I arrived in Miami. I rushed to get near the front of the line. I had the equivalent of ten dollars in my hand and gave it to the attendant to make sure there were no delays in getting me seated. Once on the plane, I found my seat. Sweat was again streaming down my face, disguising the tears that were trying to form.

As I sat there waiting for the plane to fully board, I felt my phone vibrate. It was a text from Raul.

"Beto, I'll come to the airport, don't leave." Another text followed shortly. "Please come back to the house." He obviously knew what I had discovered, and apparently the guys who followed me were members of the DCs and told him I was at the airport. "I will change everything."

"Change"? So was this part of the past from which he was trying to disengage? Was he admitting he was still involved?

I didn't answer right away. After a few minutes I sent a short text back. "I'm sorry too. I'm heading home, goodbye." Harsh, perhaps, but I still hadn't regained my composure. I knew it wasn't fair to deny Raul a chance to explain. Maybe he was over the gang. I asked myself if all of this was just bad luck—or was I really not ready to let someone steal my heart again? Maybe once I got to the comfort and security of my home, I would be able to see things differently.

As the plane ascended, I looked down as the lights of Baranquilla faded. I wanted to cry but was unable to shed a single tear. I was fortunate not to have anyone sitting next to me. I wasn't in the frame of mind to make small talk with anyone. I ordered two drinks when the cabin service started. The flight attendant recognized me from the inbound flight from two weeks previous, and she asked if I had enjoyed my stay in Colombia. I nodded and told her that she had a beautiful country, thinking, *If you only knew, honey, what I just went through.* Would I ever want to come back to South America again?

I drank the two cocktails within fifteen minutes. My eyes were finally getting heavy, and I felt sleepy. For a quick moment, before I dozed off, I thought about the argument that Emil and Matthew had at dinner months ago regarding the potential threat of gang violence in South America. Matthew certainly would seize on this to claim he suspected Raul from the start. Emil would respond that things weren't always what they appeared to be. I guessed there would be truth in both of their comments. It was no wonder that Raul remained quiet during that part of the dinner conversation. He knew he would not be able to honestly or legitimately make an argument. I was eager to put the memory of that experience behind me.

❖   ❖   ❖

When I arrived in Miami, the next flight to Las Vegas didn't depart for another four hours. *Okay*, I thought, *anything to get home.* I went to the terminal bar and ordered a vodka gimlet. In minutes, the glass was empty. "Want the same, sir?" I nodded yes.

I sent Angelo a quick text. Never knowing if he was performing or sleeping in from a late show, I didn't usually call him direct. I'd first send a text. I typed in a quick message. "In Miami … on way home. Adventure over and done … and I mean done! Let's get together soon. Wes."

PART III:
ASCENT

Thirteen:

⨀ ⨀ ⨀

Doors Close, Doors Open

his was the second time in as many months that I was returning home from a long trip. I went into the house and left my unpacked suitcase in the bedroom. As I took off my jacket, I heard a clunk on the floor. I looked down. It was the small canvas satchel that Raul gave me with the iron key inside. As I picked it up, I felt a rush of anger and sadness. I took the satchel and put it in a drawer of the table in the entryway. I went outside and took a walk around the yard, inspecting the garden and thinking about how glad I was to be home. I had begun to think that it didn't pay to go anywhere, since as of late, there had been surprises waiting for me every time I came home. But this time there were no surprises. No notes, no phone messages. I told myself this was good.

❖   ❖   ❖

I had been home from Colombia for almost two months. Raul called, texted, or e-mailed me every couple of weeks. First it was to apologize and then to plead to get back together. I know I probably should have manned up and at least talked with him and asked for an explanation. It was out of character for me to avoid resolution of a conflict. I knew that my recurring nightmare about the abduction in Colombia would never go away until I confronted Raul and made peace with his deception.

Sure, there was a possibility that Raul was sincere when he claimed he left the gang and its activities behind him, but I still found it difficult to reconcile the feelings I once had for him with the truth about his past. I decided to send him an email in an attempt to bring closure, at least for me. To be honest, deep down I wanted to know if he was okay.

Raul,

It's taken me this long to even think about communicating with you. Your deception and dishonest portrayal of who you were caused me more hurt than I've known before. Your affiliation with a group that caused great harm to my best friend in Quito made me angry and resentful. The sad part is that I was starting to fall in love with you.

I find it difficult to fathom how at one moment I could be making love to a man who was so generous and loving, but at another turn inflicted pain and suffering on others.

I've had a reoccurring nightmare ever since I left Quito. I wake up sweating, my heart pounding. The irony is that in the dream, I'm the one being abducted by the very people you call 'hermanos.' I've decided the only way I can purge this from my subconscious is to forgive you. But I won't be able to forget. I wish you could tell me that I did indeed dream everything, including the dream itself.

I hope you find some peace of mind in reconciling what you've had and what you've lost. From the short time I knew you, I am certain that you have the capacity to understand that we all suffer the consequences of our actions. If I rushed dangerously to judgment that day two months ago, I am sorry, and I must assume responsibility.

Raul, I hope the good man I saw in you prevails. I wish you well.

Wes

I received a reply from Raul within several days. His e-mail was short and reflected the pain and regret that had been haunting him since I left.

Querido Beto,

You can't imagine how I have felt knowing that I hurt you, that you felt deceived, and that I may have lost someone with whom I was certain was going to be part of my life forever. A day doesn't pass when I don't think of you. The empty feeling inside is as bad as the worst pain that I could imagine. I hope that someday we can meet face to face so that I can apologize. If for nothing else, I need to close this ugly chapter, and hope that maybe there's a chance for a new one to be written.

Un Abrazo Fuerte,
Raul

I decided not to respond right away. While I had forgiven him, the feeling of betrayal still hadn't totally subsided. I figured someday we would be able to meet again. I just didn't know when.

❖   ❖   ❖

Over the next couple of months, some positive things started to happen for me.

I received a letter in the mail from the BLM offering me a grant to facilitate a strategic plan for all BLM land management in the western United States. I kept busy, traveling to major BLM offices and visiting many of the BLM land holdings. At times I would say to myself, … *and they pay me for this?* Feeling secure in the job made Las Vegas seem more and more like home. I had become indifferent to the slot machines that were ever present in the grocery stores, gas stations, and mini-markets.

Even though my dating had been reduced to Marcus and an occasional internet hook-up I was content. My focus wasn't on romance but rather enjoying my home. Finally feeling free of the guilt, pain, and anger that I brought with me from LA, I hadn't realized until recently how those emotions had filled the house to the point where there was little room for anyone else's feelings, wants, and needs. Finally, there was enough emotional space in the house for someone else—if only there was someone.

❖   ❖   ❖

It took over a month before I heard back from Raul again. He was doing community service on behalf of a gang reduction program in Colombia. He said that even though he hadn't been directly involved in criminal acts for over ten years, the loss of my friendship was sobering. He originally thought that just distancing himself from the Diablos was sufficient. His epiphany came when he realized his affiliation had caused harm to someone he loved. He said if he had known anything about the situation with Tico, he would have used his influence with his Ecuadorian counterparts to "call off the dogs."

That alone indicated to me that it was probable he would never be able to totally escape the gang's influence. Still, he knew he had to fully disclose his past and make restitution for the pain he had caused others. Only in this way could he redeem himself. He said he prayed that some day when he finished his service in Colombia, I'd be willing to see him once again. Since he had to give up his job in the United States and its corresponding work permit and visa, there was little chance he would be allowed back into the country anytime soon. I would have to return to Colombia to see him. I knew that wouldn't happen anytime soon.

Despite the hurt, I still cared about Raul. I knew that harboring ill will and negative feelings wasn't healthy or productive. Occasionally, there were little things that would remind me of him. I smiled as I recalled the morning he noticed me struggling to peel the shell off a hard-boiled egg. He taught me that if you cracked the shell and then rolled it between the palms of your hands, the shell would fall off easily. I had used his technique ever since.

❖   ❖   ❖

Jesse and I held to our commitment to talk every week for the first month. He followed through with his medical treatment and counseling. He seemed to have adjusted to his new HIV status and decided to manage it and not let it manage him. Clay did follow up with Jesse to share the story of his own HIV struggle. Jesse told me that it meant a lot to be able to relate to someone like Clay. They ended up developing a friendship and talked on a regular basis. This was a great relief to me. As far as his marriage, Jesse didn't fare as well. He and Naomi were getting a divorce, and he moved in with a friend who was gay. Over one long weekend, Jesse asked if he could come and visit me, but he wanted to know if he could bring his roommate with him. Naturally, I said yes, and wondered at the same time if there was any significance to that request. Jesse came that weekend with his roommate, Carl. I hadn't seen Jesse so relaxed and content before. He cooked lunch and dinner all three days and talked non-stop about all the plans he had for the future. In his conversation, Jesse often used the pronoun "we." I got the drift. I was happy for him but still concerned that his life had taken such a radical turn in such a short time.

Carl seemed like a nice enough guy, but like a mother hen, I was protective of Jesse during this vulnerable time. Throughout the weekend, I'd try to find opportunities to talk with Carl and get an idea of what his aspirations were. Carl was younger than Jesse and had lived a gay lifestyle since he was nineteen. He looked and acted older than his twenty-seven years. He was short and had a build like a sparkplug. He said he played football at one of the state universities. He had reddish blonde hair styled in a buzz cut, and I could see a portion of a tattoo exposed above the collar of his T-shirt. He looked more like a rapper than the paralegal he claimed to be. He said he had been "poz" for almost five years and was doing well. I was impressed how articulate he was for his age, and he was a very thoughtful and courteous houseguest, always offering to help clean up after dinner. Jesse said nothing to me all weekend to hint at any kind of relationship with Carl, but the way the two interacted assured me they were a couple, and a happy one indeed.

After watching the two of them being affectionate with one another, I reflected on my own short interlude with Jesse many months ago. Very late one evening, I was still awake reading in the living room. Jesse and Carl were rather loud while getting their groove on in the bedroom. For a brief moment I was envious of his friend. I closed my book, smiled, and felt happy that, at least for now, Jesse seemed to have found a quiet and peaceful corner in his otherwise turbulent world. In the past, Jesse the womanizer had probably been trying to compensate for the guilt he was feeling about his attraction to men. I was still his best friend and cared enough to make sure he got to experience some of the warmth and love that I had been lucky enough to share.

A month later I got a call from Jesse.

With excitement evident in his voice, Jesse exclaimed, "DB, guess what? Carl introduced me to a friend of his who worked at one of the animation studios. I submitted some of my drawings to them and there may be an opening for an apprentice-type position. Man, this would be heaven sent if it comes through."

"That's great, J-Bones. Things seem to be falling into place for you. By the way, how are you guys doing, you know, as friends?" I asked like the doting parent.

"Carl and I are doin' great together. He's really a cool dude. You know, DB, we've talked about commitment, and we're both ready to give it a try."

Jesse paused for a moment and then continued, "I know we never talked much about me being, you know, 'gay.'" His hesitation indicated he still seemed uncomfortable with the label. "But I'm startin' to understand who I am and who I'm not. I've been confused, man, but the doc is helpin' me understand everything, and maybe even why I treated women the way I did."

I could tell that his therapy was helping him adjust to the new discoveries about himself.

I could hear Carl's voice calling him in the background. "Jesse, breakfast is ready."

Jesse said to me softly, "But it's a'ight now, DB ... and Carl's good for me."

Encouraging him, I replied, "Keep being positive, Jesse. I'm proud of you."

"Thanks, DB. You're my rock, man. Love ya, my brotha."

I wished him well and told him I'd put good thoughts out in the universe for him.

❖   ❖   ❖

To my surprise, Matthew and Clay remained separated but were still seeing one another. Clay indicated that the time apart was healthy for their tumultuous relationship. They appreciated one another more and didn't fight when they did get together. Matthew also had a brief scare with a heart problem. They got it under control, but I think it shook him up enough to change his perspective on many things. Clay said he was deep into therapy and seemed to be reconciling with his family's rejection. He was still hurt and angry but was coping much better.

They were still talking about hosting the next men's dinner, despite their separation. Angelo told me that as long as Matthew was still soaking up radiation at the power plant, he would need to be heavily medicated to attend. Of course, Emil would be the only one disappointed if his sparring partner had lost some of his bite. I promised Angelo I'd provide the medication just in case.

Clay was spending almost half of his time now in Washington, D.C., as one of the advisors for a congressional committee studying HIV/AIDS programs and benefits for minorities. He invited Angelo, Daphne, and me to his fundraiser banquet in LA scheduled around the holidays. Clay's functions received a lot of support from LA celebrities. They were always entertaining events and ones I rarely missed.

❖   ❖   ❖

Tico, my friend in Quito, had left me an e-mail. He lost his job with the newspaper as word of the scandal regarding his bar and the Diablos gang spread. A friend found him a position at the Hotel Intercontinental in Quito as a tour manager. The hotel opened up a tour office down the street. Their business expanded rapidly as the government started to invest in tourist-friendly locales in the

Amazon region, and they asked Tico to manage the office. In an ironic twist of fate, the office was built on site of his burned-out bar. Tico wrote me that sometimes, when he was alone in the office, the walls would talk to him and he would laugh out loud. He told me that he had to hire some tour guide assistants as business started picking up. One of the applicants turned out to be one of the guys from the gang who met us that night. The guy was upfront with Tico about who he was. It turned out he was going to the college in the States and was home in Quito visiting that week when his brother, a Diablo member, asked him to go out with him that night. He had no idea what they were up to when they came to see us at the bar. He hoped that by working in his tour office he could make retribution for the events of that evening. Tico was impressed with his honesty. Besides his native Spanish, he was also fluent in English and Quechua, an indigenous language of the region. Tico hired him and said he'd turned out to be his right-hand man—and more. I chuckled when I pictured him and a former member of DCs sharing the same bed. Tico seemed content for now, but I've never known him to be satisfied with the status quo.

Tico said when things settle down he wanted to plan a trip to the States and looked forward to getting a first-hand tour of Las Vegas.

The last thing he mentioned was that my friend Nareem had come back to Quito looking for work. Tico was trying to find a position for him with the tour company. When he told him that I had been in Quito and asked about him, he said Nareem couldn't stop grinning. It was nice to hear that he still had good memories of our friendship and was happy to get my contact information.

About a week later I was excited to receive an e-mail from Nareem. Even before I started to read it I felt a warm rush inside, my mind flashing back to the special sensuality he shared with me. Tico was able to hire him for a position in the tour office, and the hotel gave him free room and board in return for bartending, and helping to set up special events. Nareem went on to recount the times we spent together, and it was obvious we still carried affection for one another. He said if the hotel liked him they might be willing to pay for the six-month ESL program at UCLA next year. I thought, *Damn, LA is close enough for weekend visits. I'd love to see him again.* Just the thought of a reunion got me aroused.

❖   ❖   ❖

Emil called to tell me that his father might come to LA next year for his book signing. He was especially excited that his father wanted him to be at his side at the signing.

"Hey, Papa Bear," Emil said affectionately. "Would you come?"

"Of course," I answered. After all, I was as curious as anyone to meet his pro-boxer father.

Emil bragged, "And I can't wait to play myself in the movie version."

We laughed.

"Hey, I'll bring the photo of your dad winning the light heavyweight championship. Maybe he'd sign it for me." I said hopefully.

"Baby, he may want to sign more than just that photo." Emil laughed. "Talk with you later, Wesley."

Our conversation conjured up a vivid fantasy in my mind.

❖   ❖   ❖

Angelo quit the tour. He convinced his band to stay put for a while to record a new CD. They spent some time playing at local venues in LA, but he was tired of the late nights, the groupies who would follow the band everywhere, and the occasional obsessed fan.

One evening, Angelo called me.

Excited like a little kid, Angelo announced, "Wes, guess what? I got invited to play at the Monterey Jazz Festival in California this fall. They are going to bill me as one of their success stories, having had my start as one of their all-star high school band players years ago."

Sharing his excitement, I said, "Man, it's funny how life comes full circle sometimes."

He continued, "Would you do me a big favor and come?"

Without hesitation, I answered, "Nico, I wouldn't miss that for the world! Of course I'll be there."

Up to that time, Angelo had received a lot of notoriety as one of the up-and-coming bass guitar players of the day. Stories about him appeared in various magazines like *Jazzbeat*. He was profiled in a men's fitness magazine, *Your Fitness*, as well. Even with his grueling travel schedule, he had managed to stay in shape, working out in hotel fitness centers or running in the local neighborhoods where he was staying. Despite all this press coverage, I was touched that his invitation to the jazz festival still meant so much to him.

❖   ❖   ❖

It was the weekend. Young blood was still asleep next to me. We had gone out to see a movie the night before and sat in the back row of the theater, as usual. He was unusually affectionate that night, rubbing his leg against mine and occasionally giving me a kiss on the neck. By the time we got home, we couldn't undress fast enough. Our passionate moment ended in the usual way: cuddling closely the rest of the night. Marcus was always able to stir up the passionate and sensual spirit in me. Although I needed to wake him if he was to make it to school on time, I selfishly wanted to savor the final moments with him wrapped up in the sheets next to me. His manly scent combined with the breeze coming through the sliding door was too much. I fell victim to temptation and indeed woke him up—but to let him have his way with me.

He quickly washed up, and I made him favorite breakfast of Honey Nut Cheerios, a glass of cranberry juice, and a banana.

Normally, there was a lack of substantive conversation between us, probably marking the gap of a generation of life experiences. That morning, however, he had some news for me. He had met someone online who asked him to move to North Carolina. The guy was only a few years older and had been encouraging him to visit for some time. He said he was going to go and see what he was like. Besides, the semester was almost over, and he had never been anywhere other than Las Vegas. I figured this was why he was especially affectionate the previous evening, knowing he wouldn't see me for a while. As much as I would miss his company I knew it would be good for him to start experiencing different people and environments. He was young enough to experiment. I remember when I did much the same thing. It proved a critical stage in my own development in building self-confidence and independence. While selfishly disappointed at the prospect of losing my "young blood" and the sexual comfort he provided, I was actually happy that he was moving on, and I gave him encouragement. I had feared that one or both of us eventually would get attached and build expectations of what I believe would have been an unhealthy and short-lived relationship.

After he finished breakfast, we gave each other a hug, promising to stay in touch. I dropped him off at school in time for his morning class. He wanted to finish up the semester and take his finals. He said he would text me in a couple of weeks when he got to North Carolina.

I sat out on the patio and stared at the mountains. Saying

goodbye to Marcus was more difficult than I had expected. While I rationally knew the limits of what our relationship could be, I had found myself attached and somewhat infatuated with him. Marcus reignited some of the passion and feeling that had been missing for such a long time. I wondered if I would be able to experience those feelings again.

◆　◆　◆

After nearly ten months in the desert, I had begun to experience a shift in my outlook. We were, as Emil commented at our dinner, the products of both accidents and miracles. The past—or the "non-fiction" part of my life, as I called it—was done and couldn't be changed. Now, I wanted to do everything I could to make sure that the yet-unrealized part of my life story, the "fiction" that I fantasized about, could be written with gratifying and memorable experiences.

The next three weeks were very busy at work, so I didn't really have much time for a social life—or, for that matter, to even regret that I didn't have one. My coworkers were friendly, but I rarely socialized with them.

I received a text from Marcus. He had made it to North Carolina and gotten a job at a fast food restaurant. I was happy for him. He seemed to be making friends that were his own age, something that he seemed to lack in Las Vegas. The picture he sent me of him clowning at an amusement park with coworkers filled me with nostalgia. I did miss him, but I knew he was where he needed to be for now.

After coming home from work one evening, I got online to check my e-mail. There was one from Angelo. He didn't often send me e-mails. He preferred texting as his mode of communication. I opened the e-mail. It read,

Hey Bo.

Hope this finds you well and good. Just wanted to update you on the life and loves of A. Carbonaro ... ha ha. Actually, I'm planning on one final concert gig in Hawaii before settling down in the recording studio. I'll tell you more next time I see you. But, hey, what do you think of meeting me in Hawaii next month for some R&R? I have some loose ends to tie up the next couple of weeks but will call you. I miss you and hey, it would be good for both of us to chill for a bit. We can celebrate my final tour. What u say, Wes ... up for it? Let me know. My treat!

Best and love, Nico.

Angelo had talked about cutting back on performing, and I was glad he was about to make a change. Hawaii sure sounded nice. I could use a trip that was for pure relaxation for a change. I planned to check my calendar at work the next day to see if I could swing a week off.

❖   ❖   ❖

After some coaxing, my boss approved the time off, and I got busy getting ready for a relaxing holiday with my best friend. I went into my closet and pulled out the suitcase that I had been packing over several days. I packed light for a change: shorts, T-shirts, sandals, swim trunks, one nice outfit for dinner, and a good book. I had to be at the airport by 3:00 p.m. for the nonstop flight to Maui. After the drama in Ecuador with Tico, the radical life changes impacting Jesse, and the short-lived romance in Colombia, I figured my best bud was looking out for me and knew that I needed to relax. I was ready.

After showering and laying my clothes out for the flight, I received a short text message. It was from Angelo. He knew I took every precaution when traveling and that I'd be leaving for the airport a few hours early.

"Wes, look in the bottom drawer of your nightstand, something wrapped in a handkerchief."

What an odd message, I thought. This guy has lost his mind.

I opened up the bottom drawer to my nightstand. Angelo must have known I rarely opened the bottom drawer, where I stashed odds and ends like chargers to my cell phone and Bluetooth, as well as cables for my MP3 player. I pushed the cables and miscellaneous junk aside and saw a light blue handkerchief.

I opened the neatly folded hanky. Inside was a small baggie. As I pulled out the baggie and opened it my jaw dropped. It was his ring, the same one that he left on my bedside years ago in Chicago.

Moments later I get another text.

It was in Italian. "Bello, ti desidero." Again, those were the words he had whispered on our first date.

I stood there just staring at the phone. Perhaps it was presumptive reasoning to assume that Angelo had been desiring the same thing about which I had fantasized. It was odd. I recalled something that Raul had once told me: "Things happen for a reason. Don't be afraid of where change can lead you. Let it, and don't have regrets." Not only was that thought full of irony, considering the source, but it also turned out to be prophetic.

That evening I "flew forward" to Hawaii … and to Angelo.

Fourteen:

⑂ ⑂ ⑂

Flight of Fantasy

I had been to Hawaii many times but knew that this visit would be different. Just before I left for the airport, I received a text from Daphne wishing me a great trip. She wrote, "Wes... enjoy your trip... and btw... never heard Angelo so excited! ...like a teenager!"

Although still unsure of what it all meant, I tried not to be analytical. It had been on my mind for a while that maybe Angelo had started to think about taking our friendship to a different level. I knew we wouldn't have been able to sustain a relationship when we were younger and focused on our individual career goals. But time had passed, and I think we both realized that it was time to be honest about our true feelings for one another. I was restrained in my hope that this was his expectation too. For once, I just wanted to let things happen and see where they would lead. I went to the bar by the gate and downed a vodka gimlet. The drink was having the desired effect. I was feeling a bit high and giddy when the gate attendant announced the fight.

The flight was supposed to be full, so I figured I wouldn't have the luxury of an empty seat next to me. I boarded and found my usual seat on the aisle. The window seat beside me was one of the few open seats left. I was hoping no one would claim it. At this point, the three horrors of flying crossed my mind. They all had to do with who or what would sit next to me. They were, in no particular order: the unhappy baby with the happy mother who was oblivious that her baby was unhappy, the poster child for bad hygiene, and the nosey nelly who would repeat your responses loud enough so that everyone nearby could hear them. Just when I thought I was in the clear, a little old lady, dragging a bag as if it weighed as much as she did, stopped next to me. She was physically frail but perky and alert. She nodded as I pointed to the empty window seat. I helped her store her carry-on. She thanked me, and we buckled up for takeoff. We taxied to the runway, but the captain announced a short delay due to heavy traffic. While we sat, waiting, I noticed she had a little pad of paper on her lap and would occasionally write something down. Even though I was curious, I was reluctant to start up a conversation I might later regret. She was quiet, and I felt relieved that I seemed to have avoided the three feared candidates for bad seatmates. Once we were airborne, I was happy to see that cabin service had started. I wasn't terrified of flying, but a few cocktails helped me to ignore the fact that I was encapsulated in a sausage shaped metal tube speeding thirty thousand feet above the earth. I didn't like the feeling of confinement, so getting a little buzz on kept me distracted.

As the flight attendant pushed her cart near our row, the elderly lady next to me caught the attendant's attention and requested, "I'd like a Bloody Mary, please."

Smiling, she turned to me and asked, "Can I treat you to a round, young man?"

I chuckled, thinking, *My gosh, I'm being hustled by grandma.*

"Sure, thank you." I said.

I asked the attendant for a Bloody Mary as well and an extra bottle of vodka. The attendant smiled and probably thought it was mother and son on vacation together.

The elderly lady noticed the surprised look on my face and tapped me on the leg. "You remind me of my son. We always used to have Bloody Marys. He would fly with me back to New York where my husband lived."

"I'm Wes, by the way." I wanted to be polite.

She put her frail hand in mine and said, "I'm Claire."

"And what does your son do?" I asked, realizing that I had broken my own cardinal rule about getting into personal conversations with strange seatmates.

She quietly replied, "Oh, he passed away two years ago. He was a horticulturist in Maui and managed the gardens of one of the big resorts there. He succumbed to cancer."

She looked down and stirred her drink. "I had his ashes scattered in a special place on the island. I go every year on his birthday. I keep a little journal each time I come back."

I paused for a moment and took two big sips of my drink. "I'm so sorry. That must be difficult for you."

"Yes, it is." She stopped for a moment and sampled her Bloody Mary. "Ah, good, just the way I like them."

She continued, "Bert was my only son. I'm over the sadness now. Instead I celebrate him—and myself for having endured a long, fulfilling life with the hope that I'll continue to see many more sunrises."

The relevance of her comment wasn't lost on me. "That's a wonderful way to look at life. I'm no stranger to loss myself and am just now getting on my feet again."

She just winked in agreement and continued to nurse her drink.

I looked down at my hand and stared at Angelo's ring. I rubbed it gently with my other hand. It was too large to put on my ring finger, so I wore it on my middle finger. When he saw it, Angelo would probably make some joke that it was a fitting finger for that ring. I didn't care. I kept touching it, as if to assure myself that everything was going to be okay, that I was safe, that life was good.

Out of the corner of my eye I couldn't help but notice Claire staring at my hand.

She commented, "What a beautiful ring. I remember I gave my husband one that was very similar. It must be special to you."

Normally a comment like that from a stranger would seem forward and out of place, but for some reason it didn't seem at all inappropriate for her to make that observation.

"Yes, it is," I said as I turned, pretending to reach in the seat pocket for something. I didn't really want to have to go into detail about its true relevance, of which I wasn't entirely certain myself.

Claire, however, asked a more probing question. "Does your ring represent the past or future?"

I was a bit floored by the boldness of her inquiry, yet she seemed genuinely interested.

"Well," I said hesitantly, "probably both past and present. It's the ring of an old friend who I am going to visit in Hawaii. He left it at my house a while back and wanted me to bring it to him." Just then I realized I had given her enough information to start a wildfire of inquiries.

Claire's face had a thoughtful expression. She looked at me with a genuine smile, her eyes surrounded by wrinkles but still bright and alert. Instead of digging deeper into my business she quietly initiated what would become a more serious, philosophical monologue.

"Well, Wes, what's important is to live a life that matters. Gather all the mistakes and triumphs that you've had, acknowledge them, and then put them on a mental book shelf where you can visit them from time to time, but don't allow them to obscure your vision of the future."

She paused and glanced at the tattoo on my forearm.

"Sometimes it's good to do something radical that changes the pace, intensity, and direction of your life. You may fall several times, but when you get up, you have to take control. This resets your compass." She pointed to my forearm.

As Claire stirred her drink, I thought, *How serendipitous—here was a complete stranger sharing her life philosophy that so closely resembled my own.*

She continued, "That's what I did after I lost my son. I took a trip to Tofino, Canada, a remote spot on the coast of British Columbia. It's not a well-known location or a popular tourist destination. It's frequented only by a small group of people with a common interest, and that is to experience the thrill of violent winter storms hitting the northwest coast of the continent. I heard about this place on TV. I spent six days there and was fortunate to witness one of the fiercest storms of the winter. For three days the violent wind, rain, and surf pounded the coast. Our lodge was positioned safely on a cliff overlooking the rugged coastline and beaches. While we all knew we were safe, the force of nature was such that we still felt a primeval fear in our gut."

Claire was animated, waving her arms as she continued to describe the scene.

"The great storm passed over, and what remained was a peace of the kind I had never before felt. Like the baggage we drag through our lives, the burly driftwood and shiny shells once adorning the beach were gone. A new and higher tide swept them back to the sea, replacing them with new treasures," she said. "I'm old now. I've experienced many high and low tides."

She took a long sip of her drink and then continued to dispense her philosophy. "My experience in Tofino helped me to embrace change and be fearless facing the unknown, all the time using where I've been to help me appreciate the worth of the remaining journey. Those who avoid risk and chance do indeed avoid many of the lows.

But they also deny themselves many of the highs, and these are what make life worth living."

Claire paused as if digging deep through distant memories and fidgeted with a tiny ring on her finger. "I only wish I had come to this realization sooner in my life. My husband was a musician in New York. He was well known, but life was hard then—the late hours, the constant traveling. I wanted to settle down, but he was busy with his career. We stayed together, but I wish I had been more fearless and stuck by his side. Perhaps he wouldn't have died at such a young age."

I really didn't know how to respond, so I remained quiet.

She said one more thing, noticing my awkwardness in not responding. "Wes, I can sense something about you. I'm rather good at that, you know."

She winked. "That ring probably represents more than you realize at the moment. Let it take you to new places. Instead of spending time trying to understand the meaning of life, simply learn to enjoy the experience of being alive." She gently squeezed my hand and then laid her head back. She soon fell asleep.

We didn't talk the rest of the flight. I ordered another cocktail for myself. I wasn't sure if I comprehended her entire message, but I did sense that she had an uncanny grasp of what it was like to experience life.

I started to read through a few magazines that I had bought at the gate, but my eyes were getting heavy. I fell sound asleep. It was the announcement from the captain about our descent that woke me up. I glanced over, and Claire was gone.

I asked an attendant where she was.

"She's sitting in first class. She's a frequent flyer of ours, and we upgraded her seat." The attendant then handed me a neatly folded piece of note paper. "She asked me to give this to you when you woke up."

As I slowly unfolded the paper, a small locket hanging from a gold chain fell into my lap. I gently opened the locket and inside was a tiny compass, no bigger than a teaspoon. How ironic, I thought, as I glanced at the compass tattoo on my left forearm. She included a note:

"My late husband gave this to me as an inspiration to stay focused and on track during some of our difficult times. It has served its purpose for me. I hope it can do the same for you. You'll know when you no longer need it. Then, you can pass it on to someone who does."

It was a surreal moment.

Moments later, the captain announced our approach to the airport. I would have to try to catch Claire on the way out to thank her. As we started to deplane, I was anxious to get up to the front and see if I could catch up to her. She was nowhere in sight. This lady had swept in and out of my life like the tide she had spoken of earlier. I squeezed my hand tight to feel Angelo's ring on my finger.

Fifteen:

᭶ᣟ ᭶ᣟ ᭶ᣟ

Aloha

As I walked down the ramp toward the gate, my preoccupation with Claire was replaced with the anticipation of meeting Angelo. He had told me he would be meeting me at the gate. As I got closer to the gate, I could see him standing in the distance. Even though I wasn't completely sure what to expect, my heart started to beat like a teenager's. In all the times that Angelo and I had gotten together these past years, I had never felt like this. My knees felt like they were going to buckle, and I wondered if people next to me could hear my heart pounding.

Angelo was standing at the end of the ramp. He was wearing baggy shorts, sandals, and a flowered shirt, unbuttoned midway to reveal his tight chest and a little bit of dark curly hair. Before I could say anything, he rushed up and put a lei around my neck. He held me in a long embrace without saying a word and didn't seem to care if others were looking at us. I had hoped for a warm reception but had never expected anything like this. I had become aroused but didn't care if anyone noticed. All I wanted was to savor the moment, which seemed to unfold in slow motion.

His eyes were fixed on me and mine on him.

When he embraced me, he whispered, "Wes, I've waited for this for a long, long time." I could smell the scent of coconut butter on his skin. Although he'd shaved off the goatee, he sported a day's growth of beard. It was rough but felt good.

I looked into his big brown eyes and said, "Me too." I ran my hand along the back of his neck, burying my fingers in his darks curls.

Sometimes things didn't have to be said. I knew that our relationship had taken a sudden turn, and I was ready to be with Angelo in a way that I hadn't experienced since we dated in Chicago. I didn't really have time to process what was happening. Rather, I chose to surrender to whatever was about to unfold. It was odd that with others that I had met, like Raul, I questioned whether I was ready to get involved again. With Angelo, I entertained no such doubts. We had known one another through the ups and downs of our careers and past relationships. For a moment I thought about what Claire had said on the plane. Perhaps a new tide had brought Angelo and me back together.

Accustomed to being very familiar and demonstrative with his feelings, Angelo put his arm around my shoulders as we walked toward baggage claim. This probably reflected his upbringing in a very physical and loving Italian household. It complemented my more formal Eastern European heritage, where friends and even family were more conservative in the use of physical contact. I loved this about him.

Angelo rubbed my shoulder and inquired, "How was your trip, Wes? Are you hungry? Do you want to stop on the way and get something?" I could tell he was both excited and nervous by how quickly he talked.

Equally nervous, I told him, "Nico, I just want to get to the hotel, change, and get comfortable. We've got some catching up to do."

"Great, we can order room service. You won't believe the beach cottage I got. I had to pull a few strings to get it, but I want our week to be special." I could feel his hand squeeze harder on my shoulder.

"Hey, it's already special." I put my arm around him and could feel the muscles in his back. I just wanted to be alone with him.

In all the excitement at the gate, Angelo had just noticed the ring on my middle finger. He grabbed my hand and a giant grin grew across his unshaven face. "Thanks for wearing it, Bo."

The airport was busy and loud, and it was difficult to carry on a conversation. I went to claim my bag while he went over to one of the tour desks. He wanted to get some tour brochures. My guess was that they were for deep-sea fishing. He and his father used to go fishing in Lake Michigan when he lived in Chicago, and it had been a dream of his to spend a day out on the ocean.

After getting my bags, we headed out to the resort in the convertible Mustang that he had rented. Angelo had spent the night before at a hotel near the airport. His bags were already in the car. We made general chitchat during the drive out. With the top down and the wind rushing, it was hard to talk, anyway. Through most of the trip, Angelo had his right hand on my leg. I put my hand on his. It felt like we were boyfriends again. It was as if the long interval of years in which were just best friends had never existed.

Angelo turned off the main highway, and for about two miles, we drove down a winding and very narrow two-lane road. We finally pulled into a small parking lot. There was no big high rise or hotel building that I could see, just some thatched rooftops in the distance.

"We're here. Paradise lost, and now found." He exclaimed.

"Are you sure you're not taking me on a damn camping trip?" I joked. I still wasn't able to see any semblance of a hotel or resort.

"No, Bo. Just wait 'til you see this place. I've never stayed here, but one of the band members recommended it." Angelo was grinning like he had discovered treasure.

We walked up to the first building that had a thatched roof and no walls. There was circular desk in the middle with a lady dressed in a floor-length floral dress. He was clearly pleased with himself for finding this hideaway.

He said to the receptionist with a proud smile, "Carbonaro. I had a reservation, please."

"Welcome, sir. You're in cabana number three. It's all ready as you requested. Let us know if you need anything." The lady handed Angelo the key and smiled at us with a look suggesting she knew we were more than just friends.

As we walked up to our cabana, surrounded by mangrove trees and hibiscus, I exclaimed, "Wow, Nico! This is incredible." It was private and right on the beach. "This looks like a honeymoon suite."

With a flirtatious grin on his face, he replied, "Well, maybe I got things backwards." He embraced me and gave me a long, luscious kiss on the lips. He lips were full, and his breath was warm and fresh. When he released me, I noticed his eyes were watery.

"Wes, you don't know how long I've dreamt for a moment like this with you. I hope you're okay." He wiped his eyes.

I didn't speak right away. I just pulled his head into my chest and kissed his neck. I whispered, "I'm the happiest man on the planet right now."

We walked into the cabana. It was truly paradise. It had all the amenities: a king-size bed with a mosquito net over it, a marble bath, and a front patio with chairs that faced the ocean. There was a bottle of champagne on ice on the table next to the bed. I told Angelo I needed to take a quick shower. I think it was the quickest shower I had ever taken.

When I walked out of the bathroom with a towel around me,

Angelo was lying on the bed with nothing on. His body looked like an Italian sculpture. The champagne glasses were full. I went over to him and he pulled the towel off of me.

"Bello, ti desidero," he whispered. I melted.

We made love for most of the afternoon—not just sex, but love. All the deep feelings for one another that we had suppressed all of these years percolated up in a passionate and steady stream of lovemaking. Neither one of us said much. We didn't have to. Angelo was a romantic. He was slow and deliberate in finding all the sensual spots to please me. We took turns exploring one another, smelling and tasting what we had both longed for. It was only minutes before we both exploded on one another. Our passions had been building throughout the day and weren't about to be contained for long.

We paused only momentarily before resuming our own version of sexual healing. Like during our very first date, Angelo would look directly at me with those dark brown eyes. He was in control, and I gladly submitted. With the exception of Nareem in Ecuador, Angelo was one of the few men with whom I felt completely uninhibited. Although he was versatile in bed, we both seemed to become most excited when he would top me. We christened every part of that small cottage with our sex play. The curls of chest and stomach hair captured beads of perspiration, and his sweat carried a manly scent—strong, but pleasurable. Angelo's body was still tight and defined. When he was close to climaxing, he looked directly in to my eyes with his mouth open.

"C'mon, please, Papi," he groaned.

The veins in his arms were swollen from holding me so tightly. His rough beard rubbed against my face, exciting me to climax.

"Ahh, it's good," I whispered as his sweat dripped on my face.

My friend Nareem's phrase, "que chévere," rumbled through my mind.

We exploded together and remained in a tight embrace.

As the afternoon wore on, our room filled with the distinguishable smells of lovemaking.

Finally, we both sat up and started giggling, a little embarrassed by the fact we'd been in bed all day and were badly in need of a hot shower. We finished off the champagne. The sun was getting low in the sky, and the orange hues shining through the wooden shutters of our cabana were announcing the forthcoming sunset.

I rested my head on his shoulder. "Angelo, I'm not sure what to say right now. I'm feeling something I have never felt before. I have to ask if it's okay that I feel this way."

"Wes, I love you, and I want to be with you from this day forward." His eyes got watery again. We both began to cry. The frustration of having had repressed our feelings all those years was finally released.

Angelo continued, "You know, I always respected your relationships and wanted the best for you. Down deep, I guess I always envied those guys. I knew back in Chicago that neither one of us was ready to settle down. I guess it was a good thing we didn't try to do anything back then. It probably wouldn't have worked."

I began rubbing Angelo's chest and stomach.

After taking a final sip of his champagne, he continued, "But I did promise myself one thing, and that was if there was ever an opportunity to be with you again, I wouldn't let it pass me by. After you met Raul, I was upset that I had missed my chance. Even though he seemed like a good guy at the time, I secretly hoped it would be a short fling. I knew I needed to be with you."

He turned his head and kissed me. I didn't want his sensual lips to leave my mouth.

I replied, "I know, Nico. I felt the same way. These past ten months have been hard on me. I've made some mistakes. But it's funny, you know, how a moment like today can suddenly make all of yesterday's mistakes vanish."

I rubbed his thigh and said, "I feel like a new man, and I'm with the man I want to have in my life."

Angelo turned around to face me. "Remember, in Miami, we were having breakfast in your room and you asked me if I had ever truly been in love? You remember that?" He had an intent look on his face.

"Yeah, and I remember you never answered me," I said.

"Uh-huh, that's 'cause your damn phone rang." He laughed. "I suppose it was for the best, 'cause I don't know if I would have told you the truth. It was you, the only man I've ever had these feelings for."

His smile disappeared, and he started to get emotional again. We shared another long kiss.

We sat there for a while in silence, enjoying the moment.

After several minutes, Angelo broke the silence and said, "Wes, we need to clean up and get something to eat. I have to replenish the energy you drained out of me." He had a big grin on his face.

I said, "Hey, me too." I gave him a poke in the chest and pointed at the ring on my finger. "You see, I'm not taking this baby off like you did." We laughed. "And remind me, I need to tell you about this lady I met on the plane. It was the most unusual experience I've ever had. It was uncanny, but I'm beginning to realize she was right about what she told me."

Angelo inquired, "And you never met her before? It sounds like one of those six-degrees-of-separation moments."

I continued, "There was a connection between her and me as though we had met before. It was as if she was supposed to be there."

Angelo was putting on his boxers and was half-listening to me. "Yeah, you gotta tell me more about it, but hey, the sun is setting, come out here for a minute."

I figured there would be another time to tell him about Claire. He had already grabbed a blanket for the beach. The sun was setting and we didn't want to miss the moment. I lay down next to him. He wrapped his arm around my shoulder, and we watched in silence as the fiery Hawaiian sun made a gentle splash into the watery horizon. I couldn't help but feel that tomorrow was the start of a new life for me. At least, that was my hope. I vowed to do whatever was in my power to make that happen.

Throughout the night, the sound of the surf set a cadence for our continued love-making.

❖   ❖   ❖

Angelo woke me up early the next morning.

"Baby Bo, you need to get up. I have some special plans for today." He playfully pulled the bed sheet off of me.

"Huh, what the hell time is it?" Rolling my eyes I said, "Uh, let me guess … fishing, right?"

"Damn, how'd you know?" Angelo frowned as though he was disappointed that I guessed correctly.

I replied, "I know you pretty damn well, Mr. Carbonaro. You always talked about your dream to go deep-sea fishing. If you're going to surprise me, you gotta do better than that."

Angelo giggled. "Okay, you'll see, my sleepy friend. There's more to come."

We quickly showered. Angelo packed a small bag with some drinks and snacks, and an extra pair of short and tank top. We hopped in the car and drove about forty minutes to the marina. He checked in with the harbormaster, and we found our boat. It wasn't as large as I had imagined and could only hold eight people. Angelo said only four had booked for this trip.

We set out to the open sea. Angelo was like a little kid, excited at the prospect of hauling in a marlin or swordfish. He had already imagined it stuffed and hanging on a wall. I was tickled to see him so happy. I knew part of it was the fishing trip, but it was also having been able to share it with me.

We had been on the water for just over an hour and hadn't gotten so much as a nibble. We enjoyed the time out on the water, nevertheless. We knew we would have to be discreet about displaying affection since there were three others plus the crew on the boat. Angelo would occasionally wink at me and smile. He knew that would get a rise out of me. Suddenly, there was a tug on Angelo's line.

"Hey, Bo, I think I got one." Angelo was so excited his eyes were open wide like saucers.

He slowly started to reel it in. The captain asked if he needed help.

"Nah, I got this baby," he proclaimed with pride.

He would slowly pull up the line and reel in the slack. He was having the time of his life. Whatever was on the other end didn't put up much of a fight, although Angelo played it up as if it was the largest catch of the month.

Pretending he needed help, he called me over. "Bo, can you help me for a minute? Grab the pole."

I started to reach for it and he moved my hand to his crotch, and whispered, "This one."

We both laughed. No one was watching. They were all looking out to sea, waiting for Angelo's big catch to break the water.

Angelo smelled like cocoa butter. I wanted to grab him, but I knew I'd have to wait.

"I'll get even for that. You're gonna have to cook whatever is on the other end, okay?" I teased.

Angelo affirmed, "Sure 'nough." His tank top was soaking wet, and the sweat beaded on his muscular shoulders and arms.

After about a twenty-minute "fight," Angelo reeled in his prize, a modest twelve-pound tuna. Soon after, the captain announced it was time to head back to shore.

When we returned to marina, the captain invited everyone to a little restaurant at the far end of the pier. His wife owned it, and she was always happy to cook the day's catch for everyone. We stayed for a delicious dinner.

When we got back to our cabana, the sun was starting to set. We sat on the beach together.

I held Angelo's hand and said, "Nico, we haven't talked much about the future. I just want you to know that I want you in my life. I don't know how we'll do it with your touring, but we'll find a way."

I felt Angelo squeeze my hand. He replied, "Wes, I don't think that will be a problem. I talked to some agents, and they're trying to get me a permanent gig in Las Vegas. I'm even willing to work in a backup band for some of the shows."

He turned to me and gave me a soft kiss and stroked my head. He added, "I just want to settle down and be with you. I could spend more time in the studio and write too. Are you sure you're ready to start all over again?"

"Yes." I said. I laid my head in his lap. I didn't need to say any more.

We were exhausted from a hot day in the sun and, of course, the previous night of bed play. We went inside shortly after the sun went down and fell soundly asleep.

❖   ❖   ❖

The next morning, Angelo woke me up, trumpeting his morning announcement. "Hey, Wesley Svoboda, time to get your lazy ass up. I've got a surprise for you this morning."

"What, again? This time I don't have a clue," I said, shaking my head.

Angelo joked, "Just as it should be, Sherlock."

I peeked over the sheets. He was standing over me in his boxers. He appeared to be aroused.

I added, "Why don't you come back into bed for a few minutes, sailor boy."

I liked it when Angelo was playful. It was boyish and sexy at the same time.

Looking at me as if I was being disobedient he said, "Sorry, Bo, we're on a schedule. We need to pack an overnight bag this time."

Again, we packed up, got in the car, and headed in the direction of town.

With a look of cautious amazement on my face I asked, "Where we going, Nico?"

"Don't worry. I'll have you back by tomorrow night." Angelo reassuringly squeezed my leg.

He was having a ball planning and directing the vacation. I could tell it had been on his mind for some time.

To my surprise, we were at the Maui airport. We drove to the section where the private planes were parked next to a small terminal.

"We're here—well, not exactly. We need to take a short flight," Angelo said.

I looked at him, pretending I was concerned. "What the hell? Where are you taking me? Am I being kidnapped?"

"Yezzir, and you won't regret it," he answered. He slapped me on the butt.

We boarded a small plane that had only eight seats. Only two other passengers joined us.

No sooner had we taken off than the captain announced we would be landing on the island of Molokai in twenty minutes, one of the remotest islands in Hawaii.

I turned to Angelo and said, "Wow, Nico, I always wanted to come here." He didn't say anything. Instead, he rubbed my hand and caressed the ring on my finger.

At the tiny airport, Angelo had reserved a jeep. We drove about a half hour on the deserted highway and turned up a small dirt road. To my amazement, the road ended at the beach where a small cottage was nestled among some plumeria trees which filled the yard with their sweet fragrance.

"Nico, this is amazing. Are we staying here?"

"Yes, is that okay with you?" he said with a grin. "It's owned by one of my Uncle Nick's friends. This area of Molokai used to be a colony for artists and musicians nearly fifty to sixty years ago. Most of the buildings are gone now."

He pointed down the beach. "My elderly aunt has a tiny cottage not too far away. I never know if she'll be there since she has no phone. We can check on her later."

"Damn, you outdid yourself this time!" I exclaimed.

I was about to reach out to give him a big hug but he beat me to it. His arms wrapped around me as he pulled my head against his chest.

His smell overwhelmed the sweet scent of the surrounding flowers, and his moist skin felt cool against mine. "I love you, Wes," he said.

I answered with a kiss on his moist chest.

There were no other buildings within sight, and the broad expanse of beach seemed like it belonged to us. He had asked the caretaker to stock the cottage with food and alcohol. There was no need to leave. There were two kayaks on the beach for us to use as well. He had thought of everything.

After unpacking the few things we brought, we put on our swim trunks.

The humid but gentle breeze was soothing, and the warm ocean water felt wonderful. There was no one around, so we took off our trunks and got playful.

"Hey, don't get me started again." I pretended to complain.

"Okay, I'll give you a pass for now, but just wait 'til later." Angelo grabbed me, gave me a squeeze on the private parts, and ran back up the beach. His skin glowed in the tropical sun.

We spent a good part of the morning swimming and walking on the beach. Angelo went inside and made a little lunch. He brought it outside on the patio with a couple of beers.

While eating and sipping on a beer, he said, "Okay, now tell me more about your little adventure on the plane the other day."

I was glad he reminded me. I was so distracted by being with him that my encounter with Claire completely had slipped my mind.

"Angelo, this lady was amazing. She lost her husband years ago and more recently her son to cancer. Despite the loss, she seemed to have regained such a positive outlook on life. She said I reminded her of her son who used to work on Maui."

I took a long sip of my beer and continued. "It was the weirdest feeling. She introduced herself as if she had expected me and encouraged me to embrace change, sensing that I had experienced recent disruptions in my life."

Angelo interrupted. "And you're sure you never saw her before?" He had a questioning expression on his face.

"No, and when I woke up from a nap, she was gone. They had moved her up to first class, and I never saw her again. But get this. Before landing, a flight attendant came back and gave me a small package. She said it was from the lady who had sat next to me. It was a compass." I pointed to the tattoo on my forearm. "I tell you, it was uncanny."

Angelo's face went blank. "Uh," Angelo said with a slight stutter, "what did you say her name was?"

I replied, "Claire, but I never got her last name."

Angelo's mouth fell open. "Oh my God. Wes, finish your beer. There's something we need to do right away."

Angelo had a look of urgency on his face that I hadn't seen

before. He ran down to the beach and dragged the two kayaks down to the water. He waved for me to follow.

"Come on, there's somewhere we need to go. It won't take us long," he said.

I followed his directions but hadn't expected any more surprises. I asked him several times what was wrong.

Jumping into one of the kayaks he replied, "Nothing's wrong, Bo. There's just something we need to do. Trust me. It's okay."

I quickly got into the other kayak and followed him.

With that assurance, we paddled for about a half hour along the beach to a small inlet. As we continued a little farther, I could see a small bungalow nestled in the trees about twenty-five feet from the water's edge. Angelo started paddling toward the shore. I was worried about trespassing, but Angelo waved his hand, signaling it was okay. There was a small, dilapidated dock, but it was in too bad of shape to tie up there. Angelo paddled past and beached his kayak on the sandy shore. As I pulled my kayak up next to his, I saw someone come out of the bungalow and walk toward us. I figured, *Uh-oh, now we're in trouble.* As the figure got closer, I froze. I couldn't believe it. It was Claire.

Dressed in a flowered muumuu, Claire walked slowly down the gentle slope to the water.

After recognizing Angelo, she said, "Nico, my baby. What a nice surprise. I didn't know you were coming." She gave Angelo a kiss on the forehead. "Where are you staying, at Uncle Nick's cottage?"

"Yes, Auntie Claire. I would have told you I was coming, but didn't know how to get ahold of you. You look good, Auntie." Angelo put his arm around her small frame.

"Oh, I could be better, Nico. Time has taken its toll." Claire was carefully leaning on a walking stick.

When I heard Angelo call her "Auntie," I had to pinch myself.

I stepped forward before Angelo had time to introduce me.

"Ma'am, it's me, Wes, from the flight to Maui a couple of days ago. Remember me?"

Claire paused for a moment. "Of course. My dear, welcome to our island. What a nice surprise!"

I turned to Angelo and cocked my head to the side. "And just when I thought you were out of surprises."

Angelo replied, "Wes, I didn't expect her to be here. I had heard she was failing in health and figured she stopped coming here. I haven't seen her since her son's funeral a couple of years ago."

"Why don't you boys come up to the house?" Claire waved for us to follow her.

She walked slowly ahead of us. Angelo grabbed my hand and gave it a big squeeze as we followed her into the house.

"Would you boys like some iced tea?" We gladly accepted.

The cottage was modestly furnished. There was a set of wicker furniture and a small kitchen big enough for only one person to stand in. There were a few photos on the walls of people who I assumed were family members.

Pointing to a picture of a young man standing in a formal garden, I asked, "Is this your son, Claire?"

A little surprised that I remembered, Claire answered, "Yes, that's him. Remember, on the plane I told you he was a curator of some of the gardens in Maui? He would stay here with me whenever I visited the islands."

Claire looked at the ring on my finger and then looked up at Angelo.

"Nico, that ring looks familiar. That's the one I gave your uncle after his first album was recorded. I think he passed it on to you for your graduation, didn't he?" She looked up at Angelo as she pointed to the ring.

Angelo was a bit taken back. "Yes, Auntie, it was. I mean, it is, but it's Wes's ring now."

"I know," she added calmly, looking at me. "I can tell you both share something very special."

"Yes, ma'—" I started to say.

Claire interrupted me. "Please call me Claire, Wes."

Angelo asked Claire if there was anything we could do for her while we were there. Having two strong men around could prove helpful in such a remote location.

"Thanks, but I'm well situated here. There's little to do but enjoy the sunrise and sunset," she said.

Angelo slowly walked around the room. "Auntie, you don't mind being out here all alone?"

She answered, "Oh no. I'm content to sit and look at the ocean, and I have a small phonograph to play my records on."

Angelo glanced over at the table and noticed some tattered album covers. On top was a rather plain album cover. The simple title read, *Studio Demo, Niccolo Carbonaro, 10-28-42.* There was a faded note written across the bottom of the cover. It read, "Sweet stuff, Carbonaro. — Billy."

"You still listen to Uncle Nick's music, Auntie Claire?" Angelo was holding the album.

"Yes, it's comforting to know his spirit is in the house." Seeing Angelo holding the album, Claire continued, "You know, Niccolo used to be a studio musician in New York many years ago. He played bass guitar. I hear you're quite the musician now, Nico. You must have inherited that talent from your uncle."

Angelo nodded, somewhat embarrassed that he wasn't more familiar with his uncle's musical past.

I walked around looking at the pictures on the wall, giving Angelo and Claire some time to talk alone.

Claire told Angelo to bring the album to her.

"Nico, I'm not sure I'll have the strength to return again to this place next year. I want you to keep this record. Billy Strayhorn was in the same studio when your Uncle was recording it. He autographed the album cover for your Uncle Nick a long time ago. I know you'll cherish it as I have."

Angelo, clearly touched, gave Claire a gentle kiss on the cheek and said, "Thanks, Auntie. This means a lot to me."

Angelo held the album carefully in his arms as though it was a baby. Claire gave him some plastic to wrap around it so it wouldn't get wet on the paddle back to the cottage.

He added, "Are you sure there isn't anything we can do for you? When are you going back to New York? Can I have your address? I may be playing there in a few months, and I'd love to stop by."

"Tomorrow I'll be heading home to New York." She wrote down her address and gave it to Angelo. "I'd ask you both to stay for dinner, but I don't have enough provisions for all of us. Besides, the afternoon trade winds are picking up, and if you don't head back soon it will be hard to paddle back."

The wind started to bang the screen door back and forth.

We said our good-byes. Angelo gave her a hug and a kiss on the forehead. Claire came over to me and whispered in my ear, "Wes, I hope your compass continues to guide you. Follow your hearts."

Angelo heard what she said and winked at me.

We were both silent the rest of the paddle home.

As we pulled our kayaks back up on the beach by our cottage, I turned to Angelo. "You think that running in to your aunt Claire was meant to be? I'm feeling like we just experienced something— well, something almost spiritual."

Angelo replied, "Wes, my auntie was always a spiritual person, but not in the religious sense. She studied metaphysics and Eastern religions. She's very tuned in to the people she likes. She was probably considered a kook back in her day."

He turned to me with a more serious look on his face. "You know, Wes, I think Auntie Claire helped to validate that we were meant to get back together."

Neither one of us had much to say. We were both busy processing what we had just experienced.

We settled into our bungalow, and Angelo made dinner. He was pretty detailed with the list of groceries that he had asked the caretaker of the cottage to stock for him. He wanted to cook some fish and pasta. There was a bottle of California merlot on the kitchen counter too.

It was a great dinner. We didn't discuss Claire any more that evening. We focused once again on one another. It was another clear night. We sat on the beach and watched the sun disappear. I had built a small bonfire. The flames had died down, but the embers glowed in the slight breeze. Angelo fell asleep with his head on my lap. The dim glow of the fire cast a warm light on his tanned face. I ran my fingers through his curly black hair, thinking of how far my journey had taken me in the past few months, months in which ordinary often became extraordinary. I looked up at the stars. For a moment I thought of Kevin. What would he think about me starting over again? I already knew the answer. Kevin had met Angelo on a number of occasions. He once told me that if I ever had another boyfriend, he hoped it would be someone like Angelo. I looked up again at the star-filled sky and thought, *Kevin isn't the reason the stars shine so brightly, but he is one of the reasons I look up at them.*

I leaned down and kissed Angelo on the top of his head. I wished that the universe would let Angelo and I grow old together. I knew there were no guarantees about anything. And Claire was right. Higher tides could come ashore and wash away what is familiar and comfortable. The prospect that something so good may not last forever was a hard reality to accept.

◆   ◆   ◆

We slept in the next morning after an evening frequently interrupted by lovemaking. It was nice lying next to Angelo while he was still asleep, his body moist from the tropical air. The breeze gently blew the mosquito netting that hung over the bed. The sunlight was just starting to come through the windows. Angelo loved to cuddle, and he still had one arm around me. Careful not to wake him up, I gently moved his arm and quietly slipped out of bed.

While he continued to sleep I walked down to the beach. Hypnotized by the surf, I sat wondering from what distance each wave must have traveled to reach the end of its life on this beach. As my mind drifted into a state of euphoria and relaxation, the quick memory of Nareem caught me by surprise. Perhaps it was a sign that I was feeling a part of that natural moment. He would have approved.

After sitting there for nearly an hour, Angelo walked up from behind and wrapped his arms around me.

Overwhelmed by the smell of sex still mixed with his sweat, I quickly dismissed the memory of Nareem. I turned my head and kissed his arms that crisscrossed against my chest.

"Hey, Baby Bo. You figure out how to achieve world peace yet?" he playfully asked.

"I think this week was a good start." I chuckled, looking up at his smiling face.

Angelo pulled me around and locked his lips on mine. His kiss was slow and deep.

His stuff was poking out of his loose-fitting boxers. I gave him a squeeze and could feel him getting hard.

Without saying anything, he lay back and let me please him. The tastes that had accumulated the previous evening excited me so much that I quickly became aroused. Facing one another in a grinding embrace we both unloaded. We lay there spent, the waves washing up to our feet.

Our plane back to Maui didn't leave until late in the afternoon. Angelo cooked a little breakfast, and we spent much of the day relaxing on the beach. Before we knew it, was time to shower and pack for the return trip to Maui. He wrapped up his uncle's record and carefully put it in his luggage.

As the plane took off, I looked back down on Molokai. It seemed like such a small rock in the middle of the ocean. I wondered where Claire was. And I wondered if Angelo and I would ever make it back here again.

❖   ❖   ❖

We spent three more wonderful days in Maui. Angelo had no more surprises up his sleeve. We just relaxed, ate, drank, and showed how much we loved each other. We had been so focused on one another, and on Claire, that we never discussed our departure plans. I asked Angelo what flight he was taking back.

"I booked on the same flight as you to Las Vegas. Is it okay that I call it home now too?" He looked at me with a hopeful expression.

I grabbed him and kissed him. A few tears ran down my cheek.

He wiped my face with his hand. "It's okay. We'll be okay. We're gonna make this work."

The only word that ran through my mind was "yes."

Sixteen:

⁘ ⁘ ⁘

Sanctuary?

Angelo and I made several trips back to LA to pack up and move his things to Las Vegas. We spent a couple of months rearranging things to accommodate some of his furniture and belongings. We converted small pool house into a studio so he could practice and write. His agent found him a few dates backing up visiting artists on the Strip, and he soon gained some notoriety in town. He enjoyed the occasional change of pace but was content spending most of his time at home. We would have coffee together in the morning, and then he would spend the rest of the day writing his music in either his home studio or at a recording studio on the other side of town. He was excited about his forthcoming CD.

I had done considerable landscaping, and the once-barren acre was like an oasis, full of native trees and cacti, washes, and various sitting areas, each with a view of the distant mountains. It was a perfect environment for an artist like Angelo to relax and let his creative juices flow. We called it our sanctuary.

My work hours at the BLM had become flexible since I

had a small but dependable staff that could handle many of the administrative duties. This allowed me to cut back on my travel schedule and spend more time at home. I had wondered how we would handle spending so much time at home together, but it wasn't a problem. We could sense when we needed private time but still acted as though we were on our honeymoon. I wondered if all those years that we were apart were wasted. Then I reminded myself of what Claire said about the high tide bringing in change. I knew we were destined to come together at this place in time. I hung the little compass around my bedpost to remind me of how precious it all was.

I got an e-mail from Raul, who seemed to be in a totally different frame of mind. He was positive and excited about the work he was still doing with gang members in Colombia. The government funded construction of a youth hostel for homeless young men and asked Raul to run it. He made no mention of our unfortunate adventure. I sent him an e-mail after I got back from Hawaii, telling him about reuniting with Angelo, and he said it really came as no surprise. He recalled how we looked and acted around one another at the dinner. He wished Angelo and me the best and left an open invitation to visit him. Although I still wasn't ready to make that leap, I felt that the time would come when maybe both Angelo and I would go for a visit.

While cleaning one day, Angelo opened the drawer to the desk in the entryway. He came across the satchel containing the large, old, rusted key that Raul had given me.

"Hey, Wes, what's this key for? It looks old." He inspected it and put it back in the satchel.

"Oh, that was for an old door that I don't have anymore," I replied.

Angelo nodded. He understood it was something from the past and was comfortable to let it remain there.

❖　❖　❖

Since returning from Hawaii the nightmare that haunted me those many months had been washed out of my life by the same tide that brought Angelo and I together. The latest message I received from Raul helped to bring some final closure to our misadventure.

Angelo and I seemed to fit like a left and right shoe, a comfortable and complementary pair. What was most appealing to me about him was that his personality had many dimensions that weren't readily apparent until you got to know him. What you would initially see was a handsome, intelligent, well-informed man. Just beneath the surface, you'd discover his creative spirit and talent, particularly musically. Peel off another layer, and if he permitted, you could experience his romantic and sensitive side. And if you were really fortunate he would let you dig deep enough to ignite his naughty and sensual nature.

I knew realistically that nothing was perfect or forever. I just didn't think forever would be challenged so quickly.

One evening, after we had been back from Hawaii for about two months, I came home from work. Angelo had left a note on the kitchen counter.

"Wes, come to the studio."

I thought maybe he wanted me to hear some of the new tracks on his CD. I went to the casita. Usually I could hear music playing as I approached but it was quiet inside. As I opened the door I saw a candle burning, and Angelo was sitting on a small sofa with a drink in his hand.

Angelo, in a daze, looked up. "Wes, read this." He handed me a crudely written note. "It was sent to the studio where I record. I've been sitting here all day trying to figure out what to do." Angelo's demeanor was as solemn as I had ever seen it, and I could tell he had smoked more than his usual "inspirational" dose.

I unfolded the note. It read,

Angel, you know that God has meant for us to be together.
When I watch you play I can feel your music wrap around
me like an embrace. I know this is what you want too, and
don't worry, I won't let anyone get in the way and keep us
apart. Your eternal love, PZ.

"Damn, is this from one of your groupies?" I asked.

"Yeah, I assume it is. Scary, huh?" Angelo stared at the floor.

I sat next to Angelo. "Babe, we'll be okay. This person is obviously
nuts and, hopefully, will go away and forget about you. "

Shaking his head, Angelo replied, "Wes, I wish I could feel more
confident about that being the case. You see, there are women—and
some men, for that matter—that follow us and harass us. I've seen
how obsessive some of these fans get. No, they're not in their right
mind, but they can be dangerous."

He took a sip of his drink. "Remember what happened to Grant
two years ago?"

Grant was Angelo's drummer in UnderFunk. He was a hot
guy—straight, but he always played in his jeans and tank top. He
had the women screaming and jumping up on stage during his solos.
One evening as the band was breaking down, a woman jumped on
the stage with a knife and lunged at Grant. She was screaming, "If
I can't have you nobody will." The other band members subdued
her before she got near him. She was later arrested and jailed in a
psychiatric ward of the state prison.

"Yeah, I remember. Listen, did you call the police? Do you
have any idea who this is?" I was starting to take the incident more
seriously.

"I called them. They were already here to do a report and evaluate
the letter. They said without a description or some other evidence,

there probably wasn't much they could do other than document the incident. You know, at least this house is fenced and gated. We need to start using the alarm system."

Rubbing the back of Angelo's neck, I said, "Nico, maybe you shouldn't go to the recording studio anymore."

"Wes, I'm not worried about me as much as I am about you. The fool said she would stop anyone who got in her way. That could be you, Wes."

"I doubt anyone knows who I am, at least by name. Hey, we'll be okay," I said, trying to convince myself that I believed what I was saying. He rubbed my hand and caressed the ring on my middle finger.

I continued, "Remember what Claire said when we asked her if she was afraid living alone in that house, so far away from anyone? She said, 'Boys, fear is a key that opens harm's door.' Remember that, Angelo?"

He nodded. "Yeah, she was a strong and fearless woman."

Still visibly shaken, he said, "Hey, let's go inside. I could use a little TLC to take my mind off of this." Angelo slowly got up, but his body seemed limp and drained of energy.

I grabbed his hand and led him to the house. We went right into the bedroom, stripped down and crawled in bed. For the longest while, we just cuddled. I hadn't grown tired of his sweet scent. I wanted him that night, but I knew he was exhausted. I let him fall asleep with his arm around me. I was happy just to have him at my side.

Seventeen:

♩♩ ♩♩ ♩♩

Bel Cielo

That fall, Angelo performed at the Monterey Jazz Festival in California. It was one of his proudest moments, and I was glad I was there to share it with him. One of the pieces he played was from his Uncle's demo album that Claire had given him. It was called "Beautiful Sky"—or "Bel Cielo" in Italian. Angelo rearranged it and played it at the festival with a dedication to Claire and his uncle Niccolo. It was a stellar moment.

We wondered from time to time how Claire was doing. We had no way to contact her since she didn't have a phone. Angelo sent her a short note in the mail but never got a response. His schedule in Las Vegas got so busy that he never was able to make it back to New York. A month later, Angelo's mother called and told him that Aunt Claire had passed away and, per her wishes, was cremated without a ceremony. I remember that day after hearing the news I went into our bedroom and took the compass Claire gave me off the bedpost. I put in on the fireplace mantel and lit a candle next to it. It was my way of remembering her.

A few weeks later I received a certified letter in the mail. It was from a law firm in Hawaii. I opened the envelope wondering if Angelo and I had done something wrong on our visit. The letter read,

To Messrs. Angelo Carbonaro and Wesley Svoboda. It was the last wish of Mrs. Claire Carbonaro before her death that title of said property in Molokai, Hawaii, be transferred to both of your names as joint tenants in common. The probate of the estate will take place rather quickly. Please notify this office at your earliest convenience.

I ran out to the studio where Angelo was practicing.

"Angelo, look at this. It just came in the mail." I handed it to him.

He read it and didn't say anything. He folded up the paper and looked at me, his eyes intense.

"Bo, this is incredible. Now we really have a place to call our sanctuary. We need to fix the place up. It will not only honor her and my uncle, but also create a place for us that will be private and special, only for us."

I put his head in my arms and rubbed his neck. I didn't have to say a word.

We made plans for fixing up the cottage. Although the kitchen and bath needed upgrading, we wanted to preserve its sense of history—especially the memory of his auntie Claire and her family. After another two months, probate closed, and we were able to schedule a trip back to Hawaii. It was exciting to be going there to start building and sharing something that touched both of us. It would be a melancholy trip with the realization that Claire wouldn't be there. We prepared ourselves for arriving at an empty house with only her spirit present.

❖   ❖   ❖

We rented a four-wheel-drive truck after hearing that the road to the house was unpaved and unfit for a car. It was a beautiful day when we arrived. A rain shower had just passed, and the air was moist and fresh. We saw the mailbox at the entrance to a long drive. In faint letters the name "Carbonaro" was visible.

Angelo sighed when he saw the mailbox. "We're going to continue a tradition, Wes. Let's get started."

We parked in back of the cottage and walked around to the front. It looked exactly the same as I remembered. There was little left of the old wooden dock. The rotting wood was no match for the storms and high tides of the past few months. We walked up to the front door. The screen door hung off the hinge and swung gently in the slight breeze. Angelo grabbed my hand as we walked in together. It seemed like a symbolic moment as we crossed the threshold, another marker in the young relationship that Angelo and I shared.

Angelo turned to me and pulled something out of his pocket.

"My Baby Bo, I wanted to give you a ring of your own that would hold memories of this moment." Angelo's eyes were moist as he spoke.

It was a beautiful silver band with a row of diamonds. It fit perfectly.

I leaned over and gave him a long, deep kiss. His strong arms pulled me against him. Our embrace lasted a full minute. We didn't have to say anything.

Finally, I took off his ring that I still had on my middle finger and slid it on to his.

"There, Nico, the cycle is complete again. I love you, baby."

Tempted to climb in bed and get busy, we laughed and agreed to postpone our celebration until later.

We both felt the presence of Claire as we started to clean up and organize her things. Claire wasn't the best housekeeper. It was clean, but nothing was in a particular place. It was a free-for-all of books, records, and magazines scattered about with knickknacks and memorabilia from her husband's music career. The chaos in the room reflected her free spirit. Angelo and I were both rather compulsive when it came to eliminating clutter and putting everything in its proper place. We agreed we would memorialize her free spirit by reserving one corner of the living room for a collection of her "stuff." We laughed about it, agreeing that Claire would have found it amusing.

We spent just over two weeks cleaning and painting. We hired someone to put on a new roof and rebuild the dock. Angelo hired a contractor in town to do a minor remodel of the tiny kitchen and put in new bath fixtures. He left him a key since it would take him a month or more to get the fixtures and complete the installation work. We put a fresh coat of paint on the old wicker furniture and left some of the pictures of his Auntie Claire, her son, and her husband on the wall. We agreed to name the cottage "Bel Cielo" after the composition in his uncle's studio album.

It was only a few days before we were to leave when Angelo made a discovery. In one of the bedrooms, there was a set of drawers built in the wall. We both had thought the other one had gone through and cleaned them. When I told Angelo that I hadn't looked there, he opened the top drawer.

Moments later he let out a scream. "Wes, look what I found in the drawer." I thought by this time I would be getting used to his surprises, but I ran into the bedroom ready for almost anything.

Inside was a bundle of papers tied with a ribbon. He took them out of the drawer and untied them. It was sheet music transcribed by hand. The pages were old and fragile, and the brown corners were starting to disintegrate. In bold handwriting on the top of the first page was written "'Il Mio Dolce' by Niccolo Carbonaro."

"Wes, this is music written by my uncle that was never finished. I think it means 'My Sweet One' or something like that. It doesn't look like he ever finished it. And look …" Angelo pointed to the small handwritten note scrawled on the side of the page.

"Dedicated to my sweet love, Claire."

Angelo gently rubbed his hand over the aging sheet music. "Wes, I'm going to take this home and finish it. But I'm going to dedicate it to you."

I gave Angelo a big, wet kiss. He held on to me and didn't let me go. I was hoping that it would always be like this.

When we left Molokai for home that week, we promised ourselves that we would try to escape to the island at least three or four times a year. While we had called our Las Vegas home "sanctuary," little had we realized that Bel Cielo would end up being the real sanctuary.

Eighteen:

᭶ᴵᶥ᭶ᴵᶥ᭶ᴵᶥ

Passing the First Test

We were both on a high the entire trip back to Las Vegas. Angelo spent a good part of the flight making notes on his uncle's sheet music of "Il Mio Dolce." I would look over at him occasionally and could see how proud he was, not only of the thought of being able to finish the composition, but also of the turn his life had taken.

After arriving at Las Vegas's McCarran International Airport, we caught a taxi to our place on the northwest side of town. It was nice to have a quiet place like ours to come home to, although nothing would compare with Molokai.

As the taxi neared our driveway, I could see several Metro Police cars in front of the house. Our gate to the driveway, which was normally closed, was wide open. We jumped out of the taxi, almost forgetting to pay the driver.

Angelo beat me to the front door. "Officer, what's going on here?"

"Who are you?" interrogated the officer.

"We're the owners. What's happening?" Angelo answered abruptly, irritated by the officer's indifferent tone.

At first reluctant to say much, the officer replied, "Your neighbors reported a break-in. They saw someone they didn't recognize leaving your house carrying a small box."

"Oh my God. Did you catch the person? What did they look like?" Angelo asked.

Still filling out paperwork, the officer initially ignored Angelo's question.

Angelo, starting to get a little crunchy, asked again.

The officer responded, "We just got a report that a unit picked up a suspicious individual and child walking down the boulevard. She had a small box."

"Officer, let us put our stuff in the house, and we'll be right back." I grabbed Angelo, who was still frustrated at the officer's lack of information.

"Angelo, come inside with me for a minute. We need to check what's missing, if anything."

We ran through all the rooms and took a quick inventory of anything that was obviously missing or disturbed. Everything in his studio seemed in place as well.

We hadn't found anything until I heard Angelo yell, "Oh, shit!"

I ran into the family room. He was standing by the fireplace mantel where we had many framed pictures of us, family, and friends.

Angelo was shaking his head. "Wes, look, all the pictures are knocked over, and the ones of me are missing."

"And there's something else. This pink scarf was hanging over the edge of the mantel." He was squeezing it as if he was trying to choke something. His face was getting red.

"Wes, let me see." I looked closely at the scarf. Embroidered in the corner were the initials "PZ."

Angrily grabbing the scarf out of my hand, Angelo said, "Wes, I think I may know who this belongs to. "

He stormed out of the house and walked out to the driveway where the police officer was still standing.

"Officer, we found a number of photographs missing, and we found this scarf in the house. I have an idea who—"

The officer interrupted Angelo. "They retrieved the box containing photographs. The suspect's ID says 'Pinkie Zee.' Do you know her?"

Angelo put his arm around me. "Wes, remember the lady who mailed me that threatening note a month ago? She signed it 'PZ.' I'm sure it's her." He shook his head in disgust.

Angelo answered the officer, "I think she may be one of my crazy fans. How did they get in the house? The front door was still locked."

The officer responded, "The suspect's six-year old child admitted that he crawled through the doggie door and opened the sliding patio door for his mother."

I kept the original doggie door that came with the house anticipating that I'd eventually get a dog. I suddenly wished I had.

It turned out it was that same lady. Angelo later recalled that there was a woman who often came to watch the band, and she always wore something pink. PZ was eventually charged and spent some time in the psych ward of a state facility. Nevertheless, it shook us up and reminded us of how easily life's equilibrium could be disrupted. Angelo and I never forgot that incident. While the feeling of having been violated was hard to dismiss, we were able to put the incident in perspective. This was the first problem we faced together, but it was still our home, and we wouldn't have traded it for anything else.

❖　❖　❖

Our lives didn't take long to return to normal. The BLM laid off several workers because of budget cuts, but I managed to dodge the bullet. Angelo finished his uncle's piece, and he scheduled the debut of the composition at a jazz club in Chicago, where his parents could be present. His father wasn't in good health, and Angelo wanted him to hear it since it was his brother's work.

I flew back to Chicago with Angelo for his concert.

His mother embraced me when she saw me. "Bambino mio. You still look like a little boy. Is my Nico taking good care of you?" She obviously knew and accepted our relationship, which made the reunion all the sweeter.

His performance was moving and the one-hundred-fifty-plus fans that filled the jazz club were on their feet. The reviews in the paper raved about his performance. "Hot new guitarist and composer!" "Carbonaro's bass playing rates a ten!" "Angelo Carbonaro plays a magical guitar in a composition that every lover will want to share with his or her mate." His father was clearly moved. He jokingly denied that he ever discouraged Angelo from taking guitar lessons.

On the flight back from Chicago, Angelo spent much of the time going over other sheet music his uncle had left behind in the Molokai cottage. At one point, I leaned over and teased him. "I never anticipated becoming the first lady of a big-time jazz celebrity."

Playfully, he turned and quipped, "Well, then, if that makes me the head man, I have a proclamation to make. I'm overdue for some of that sweet stuff you got, and you're in trouble when we get home."

"Okay, Mr. Man. I'll be ready for ya." I jabbed him in the ribs and gave him a flirtatious look over my reading glasses.

He reached under the armrest and placed his hand on my leg. Before I knew it, he dosed off, his head resting on my shoulder.

We returned home, relieved to find that our house had suffered no indignation at the hands of any obsessed fans.

After unpacking, I made us each a drink, and we went out by the pool and shared a lounge to watch the sunset. Typical of desert nights, the heat of the day had subsided into a warm balminess that I found sensual and seductive. As darkness came upon us, the stars shimmered from heat rising from the desert floor. Angelo lay with his head on my chest. I could smell the cocoa butter in his hair. The muscles in his back twitched as he moved his arm to caress my shoulder. It didn't take long before I became aroused. He could feel me getting hard beneath him.

Neither of us said anything. He got up and pulled off my shirt and shorts. Leaning over to kiss me I could see his erection emerging from his shorts. He stripped down and stood over me so I could service him. I put my hands around his narrow waist and ran my fingers down between his firm cheeks. After Angelo was spent he kneeled and kissed me from top to bottom. He didn't have to wait long for me to return the favor. Afterward, we cuddled face to face, letting the warmth of the evening be our blanket. We drifted off into a dreamy sleep in which we seemed to be both physically and emotionally bound together.

Nineteen:

⑊ ⑊ ⑊

Las Vegas, Nevada—Present Day

T he clock on the nightstand is still flashing, but it's now 8:15 a.m. The desert breeze continues to flow through the open sliding door, waving the sheer curtains like flags. I still have the little compass in my hand, and it's bringing back all the memories of the past year. I reach above me to hang it back on the bedpost.

Angelo is still lying next to me, his warm backside pressing against my chest and stomach, my arm wrapped over his shoulder. He slowly rolls over on his side and opens his eyes halfway. He doesn't say a word but gives me a little wink. If this is a dream, I don't want to wake up. But it isn't. It's real, and it's crazy good. The diamonds in the silver band on my finger sparkle in the morning light. Angelo's a loving and selfless man, and I intend to make sure he knows how much he is loved and appreciated. Even though I'm acquainted with the necessary care and feeding of creative egos like his, he makes no demands of me. When the end does come, I want each of us to be able to say that he loved and was loved.

I recall something that Claire told us that day we met her.

"Remember that our lives are shaped by little twists of fate that open various doors. It's up to us to decide which ones we close and which ones we walk through. Choose those doors wisely."

I realize those doors could be put in motion at any time by Tico, Nareem, or Oliver south of the border; Jesse or any one of the usual suspects at the annual dinner; another obsessed fan; or perhaps a stranger who might drift into our lives on a future tide. I've learned that the past doesn't always stay in the past, and "forever" is an often-misleading notion of the future.

All we are certain of is that we have to endure whatever falls and missteps we encounter, turn mistakes into wisdom, and face it all in one direction: forward.

Epilogue

〜 〜 〜

Leaping like a jackrabbit, the topless jeep speeds along a remote dirt road. There are moments when the bright sunlight pierces through the rainclouds that intermittently pour down on us, bringing welcome relief from the hot sun. Keeping his hands on the wheel, he occasionally looks over to check on me. He's unshaven and wears a khaki cap and sunglasses. His camouflage shorts reveal his strong, hairy legs. His green tank top is soaking in sweat and clings to his taut body. On his right shoulder is a tattoo with the letters A and W intertwined. He yells something at me, but we are traveling so fast that it's hard to hear what he's saying.

Suddenly, the jeep slows down. We turn off the main road down a muddy path just wide enough for the jeep to pass. As we come to a stop I can see the small bungalow. It's a welcome sight.

We run toward the house. I don't look back. This time, instead of the sound of gunshots, I hear loud booms of thunder approaching. Under the shelter of the front porch, we hear the big drops of rain making a loud *ping ping* on the tin roof. The sound is comforting.

He doesn't hesitate to pull me close to him.

His moist lips parting to meet mine, he softly says, "Happy one-year anniversary, Wes. I love you, still."

The smell and touch of my man overwhelms me.

This time I don't have to try to wake myself. It's real, and I can speak.

"I love you too, Nico. Welcome home to Bel Cielo."

Angelo unlocks the front door and goes inside. I stay out on the porch watching the storm pushing the high tide closer to the cottage.

My cellphone vibrates and I notice there are some text messages. One is from Daphne.

"Happy Anniversary, boys. Love you both!" It makes me smile.

I shake my head in surprise as I read the other text. It's from Nareem.

"Wes … I comes to Los Angeles for study ingles. Many loves to you … Nareem."

I stand motionless for a few moments, digesting his news.

Angelo returns and embraces me from behind.

I feel his warmth breath in my ear as he whispers, "Bello, ti desidero."

The word "yes" rolls off my tongue without hesitation.

Squeezing his hand and holding on to him tightly as if to keep from losing my balance I stare out towards the ocean and the incoming tide, wondering …

END